THE GiRL WHO LOST a LEOPARD

THE GIRL WHO LOST a  LEOPARD

NIPPERSINK LIBRARY
RICHMOND ILLINOIS

NIZRANA FAROOK

PEACHTREE
ATLANTA

Published by
PEACHTREE PUBLISHING COMPANY INC.
1700 Chattahoochee Avenue
Atlanta, Georgia 30318-2112
PeachtreeBooks.com

Text © 2022 by Nizrana Farook
Cover image © 2022 by David Dean

First published in Great Britain in 2022 by Nosy Crow Ltd.
The Crow's Nest, 14 Baden Place
Crosby Row, London SE1 1YW

First United States version published in 2023 by Peachtree Publishing Company Inc.

Composition by Lily Steele
Imported by Zoie Konneker

Printed and bound in March 2023 at Thomson Reuters, Eagan, MN, USA.
10 9 8 7 6 5 4 3 2 1
First Edition
ISBN: 978-1-68263-581-0

Library of Congress Cataloging-in-Publication Data

Names: Farook, Nizrana, author.
Title: The girl who lost a leopard / Nizrana Farook.
Description: First edition. | Atlanta : Peachtree, 2023. | "First published in Great Britain in 2022 by Nosy Crow Ltd." | Audience: Ages 8-12. | Audience: Grades 4-6. | Summary: Twelve-year-old Selvi loves the animals that live on the mountains behind her home, particularly the beautiful golden leopard, Lokka, and she is determined to protect him from the hunter Jansz who both threatens not only Lokka, but Selvi's family as well.
Identifiers: LCCN 2022056187 | ISBN 9781682635810 (hardcover) | ISBN 9781682635827 (ebook)
Subjects: LCSH: Leopard--Juvenile fiction. | Human-animal relationships--Juvenile fiction. | Hunters--Juvenile fiction. | Animal rescue--Juvenile fiction. | Sri Lanka--Juvenile fiction. | CYAC: Leopard--Fiction. | Human-animal relationships--Fiction. | Hunters--Fiction. | Animal rescue--Fiction. | Sri Lanka--Fiction. | LCGFT: Novels.
Classification: LCC PZ7.1.F36753 Gi 2023 | DDC 823.92
[Fic]--dc23/eng/20221122
LC record available at https://lccn.loc.gov/2022056187

To my nieces,
Simra, Naadira, Salma,
Zahra, Zamra, Zaeema,
Nabeeha, Heba

And my nephews,
Waleed and Yussof

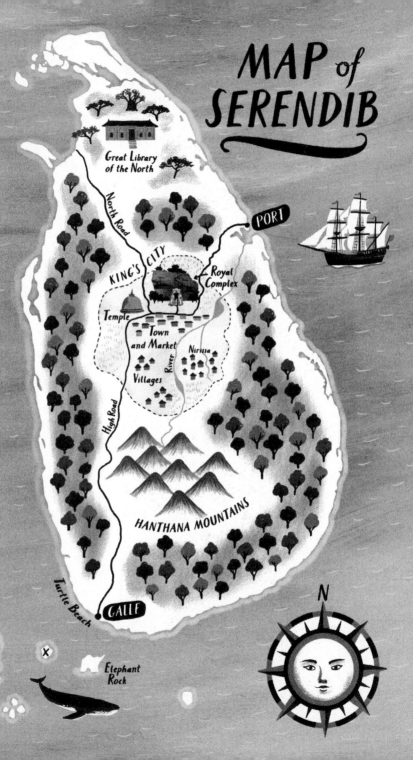

Chapter One

Selvi frowned as the man with the bow and arrow took aim at something in the bushes. She bent low and watched him from her hiding place. What was he hunting?

A whistling thrush called from a tree above him, taking off in a flutter of sleek, dark blue. The man twisted in place slightly, as if following a moving target, one eye narrowed in line with the nocked arrow. Next to him, partly obscured by trees, two other figures watched silently.

Far above him in the mountains, Selvi crouched down further. What was going on? She knew the man with the bow by sight, though only vaguely. Jansz was a large man with a big head and chipped teeth, and he and his two companions were known for being troublemakers. If Selvi's mother were here she'd tell her to stay away from them.

From her vantage point, Selvi had an eagle's view of the mountain range. Misty green hills rose around her to varying heights, all covered in a thick wilderness occasionally broken up by exposed rock. Tall eucalyptus trees shot upward like arrows from the slopes, their balmy fragrance sharpening the breeze. On her right and away to the south lay a vast plain of velvety grassland.

The man exclaimed angrily and lowered his bow. He moved toward the others underneath the tree. Whatever he'd been aiming at, it was gone now.

The men's voices drifted up, and it sounded like an animated discussion was going on. Selvi ran light-footedly toward the other side of the mountain, anklets jingling softly. They wouldn't see or hear her here, as long as she didn't make too much noise. She would scale down this side of the mountain and be away from them.

Selvi set off climbing down the bare rock face. She was adept at this. Even the dangerous climbs that no one else could manage. She was small and light, and that helped as she gripped the rock.

She'd learned to climb by instinct, feeling the sun-hot surface with her feet and arms as she used every hand- or toehold to help her down. She knew the type of vines to hold on to, the tufts of bracken that could take her weight best. Her toes curled into foliage and grasped on, as agile as the toque macaques that swung around these parts.

She was partway down the rock face when a movement below caught her eye. She paused and looked down. A clump of yellow daffodil orchids swayed softly among their pointed grassy leaves. Could it be . . . ? Her heart soared. But no, she hadn't seen Lokka in over two weeks. Maybe he'd moved on? It made her sad, but he was a wild animal after all. She shook her head and turned back to the rock face. But then she caught the soft swish of trees and knew that something was definitely moving below. She held her breath and suddenly caught a glimpse of a sinewy figure, with a hint of gold, rippling past the foot of a keena tree.

Selvi smiled broadly, her heart singing in her chest. The familiar powerful body, the glossy golden coat with dark rosettes and dabs of softest orange in them. Lokka! She'd missed him so much and was glad to see him sloping around the mountains again.

A whisper floated up in the breeze. Selvi froze as a sudden, appalling thought came to her. The men were being very quiet now. *Too* quiet. She scaled back up the rock quickly and crawled to the edge she'd been on before, anklets jingling and elbows scraping the rough ground.

All of a sudden, several things happened at once. An arrow whistled through the air into the bushes. A loud roar from an angry animal echoed up the mountains, followed by a crashing sound coming from the bushes.

Lokka!

Chapter Two

Selvi screamed. They were shooting Lokka! Her dear, strong, magnificent leopard!

The noise echoed over the mountains, reverberating from all sides. The men looked up in alarm.

Selvi fell backward and scrambled to her feet. One of the men pointed and shouted something indistinguishable. She picked herself up, her heart in her mouth.

The man was now racing up the

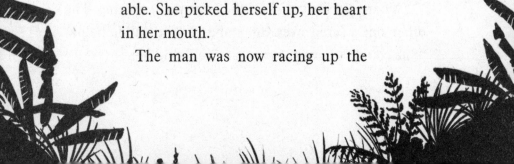

mountain toward her. Selvi started to scramble back down the rock face again. What were the men doing?! Everyone knew that hunting leopards had been strictly outlawed by the queen. The men would be punished severely if they were caught.

Which explained why they were so keen to find her.

Before the men reached the summit, Selvi had made it to the ground, dropping onto a patch of striking purple binara flowers. She thundered down the slopes, anklets jingling as her feet raced through scratchy ferns. But what about Lokka? Could he have been injured? Or worse? She shoved the thought out of her mind. No! He was quick and strong. She'd have to go and find him later and check that he was all right.

But for now, she had to save herself.

She stopped momentarily to rip off her anklets. She held the bells tightly in her fingers to muffle the sound as she ran on.

Two men were hurtling down the slope behind her and soon they'd be close enough to see her. Selvi crawled quickly under a low bush. She held her breath as the men stopped nearby, gazing intently over the mountains.

"Where did she go?" said the large man, panting. The other one peered over the slopes to the valley below. "She couldn't have got very far. We'll find her."

Selvi shrank back as Jansz's massive feet passed close to the bush.

"We'd better!" he snapped, infuriated. "I can't believe we didn't get that stupid leopard again. And I don't want the girl yapping to anyone."

Didn't get the leopard. Selvi exhaled and closed her eyes. Lokka must have escaped. Which was more than she could say for herself . . .

Jansz hollered to the third man, who was skittering down the slope toward them. "We must find her before she gets home!"

"I can't see her," he replied, holding a hand over his eyes as he scanned the area.

"She'll be hiding close by then," said Jansz. "Spread out around the mountains. We'll get her."

Selvi craned her neck to see one of the men pick up something from the ground.

"Look what I've found!" There was a tinkling as the man threw the small object to Jansz, who caught it in one hand. He held it up—a short chain with a jingling bell at the end.

Selvi shivered and opened her fist. There was only one anklet clutched in her palm.

"I know who this belongs to," said Jansz. "I'd recognize that annoying sound anywhere. It's Selvi."

Chapter Three

A wave of panic washed over Selvi. They knew her! She'd seen Jansz around the village but didn't think he'd recognize her or know her name. That meant he knew where she lived, or could find out. She stiffened, thinking about Mother alone at home.

"Let's comb the area," said Jansz. "We need to speak to her and make sure she doesn't say anything. If she's difficult, we'll just have to talk to the family a little."

Selvi shivered. She knew what that meant. *Talking* was code for something altogether more threatening. She had to protect her mother from Jansz and his thugs.

The men had split up now, and were moving slowly through the mountains. She didn't want to bump into them. She didn't want to leave them to hurt Lokka either.

Selvi peeked out from the bush again. The men seemed to have moved on a little. She watched as one of them headed away from her down the hill.

Quietly, she crept toward the path leading to her village below. It was a winding mountain track, cool and rain-washed, overhanging with tree ferns and with a sharp drop on one side. It was really hard to see if anyone was coming toward her or approaching from behind. She stumbled and brushed against some over-hanging ferns, and a shower of water fell on her.

"Did you hear that?" came Jansz's voice. "That way!"

Selvi changed direction and ran nimbly along a small path that wound steeply upward. She made it to the top, panting with the effort. To her surprise, there was a house standing in the center of a neatly swept yard under a large neem tree.

Thankfully no one seemed to be home and the front door was closed. She ran toward the back to find some-where to hide.

Jansz's voice drifted up from the path below, the trees muffling the sound. "Where did she go now?"

Selvi crept to the back door and pressed herself against it. They wouldn't be able to see her from their position and she couldn't see them either. She prayed they wouldn't notice the little winding track.

"She has to be here! Must be hiding somewhere."

Selvi shivered in her hiding place. The sound of the men's feet swept far and near. A couple of times they came heart-stoppingly close to the bottom of the path, but then they receded again.

Just when she thought they'd moved away and she was readying herself to leave, she heard the sound of light footsteps in the front yard.

Selvi swallowed a scream and flattened herself against the roughness of the back door. The footsteps started to speed up, and suddenly a person rounded the corner of the house and appeared right in front of Selvi.

It was a boy about her age. He stopped short and let out a yelp of surprise.

"Shh!" whispered Selvi fiercely, recognizing him. He was a boy from school, Amir. And, just her luck, one of the mean ones. She guessed that this was his house. "Keep your voice down!"

He stared at her in astonishment. His meanness seemed to have deserted him due to shock. "Why?" he said.

"Just please do," she implored, before he talked too much. The men might be lurking close by. Then more politely, and by way of explanation, she whispered to him, "I don't want people to know I'm here."

"What people? There's no one around," said Amir, although thankfully he'd dropped his voice.

He frowned suddenly and, much to Selvi's horror, said, "Oh wait, who's that?"

Labored footsteps sounded at the front of the yard, as if someone were trudging up the track.

It was one of the men!

Amir went and stood at the side of the house, watching where the top of the track came up to the front yard. Selvi was immobile with shock.

"Hey, boy," the man said, his voice shaky from the climb. It was Jansz! He was here, just feet away from Selvi. She couldn't see him from where she stood, but she sensed the urgency in his voice. "Have you seen a girl run this way?"

Chapter Four

Amir's eyes swiveled immediately to look at Selvi, cowering in the doorway. Selvi shook her head hard.

Jansz came closer. Selvi could hear him now, breathing heavily, though he was thankfully still hidden by the side of the house.

"Well?" said Jansz to Amir. "It's not a hard question, is it? Have you seen her?" Amir just stood there, his eyes darting all about the place as if wondering how to answer.

"I have a coin if you've seen anything useful for me," said Jansz, and he must have shown Amir something that made his face light up.

No! Selvi mouthed. *Please don't.*

Amir dragged his eyes away from Jansz and scratched his head. "Er, no. I haven't seen any girl. But I'll keep an eye out."

Selvi closed her eyes in relief.

"Good," said Jansz. He shuffled off, his footsteps rustling slowly down the track.

Selvi stood motionless for a while until all sounds of him had died away. She felt faint with relief once he was gone. She leaned her head back on the door and looked up, exhaling noisily.

"Thank you," she said to Amir, who was scuffing his toe on the sandy ground.

"What does he want with you?" asked Amir.

Selvi hesitated. She didn't really want to tell him, but she felt she owed him an explanation. "I saw him and his thugs try to kill a leopard."

Amir's eyes goggled. "Out here?"

Selvi nodded. It was acceptable to kill leopards that strayed into villages and posed a threat to humans, but going out to the wilderness to hunt one was a punishable offense.

He looked thoughtful for a moment, then shrugged and moved to stand in front of her expectantly.

"Is there anything you want?" she asked, confused.

He pointed to the door behind her. "Just to get into my house."

"Oh, right." Selvi blushed and moved aside.

Opening the door, Amir gave her a half-smile and went inside. Since it was safe to leave, Selvi went around to the front of the house and made her way back down the tiny mountain track. Trees of twisty branches lined one side, their trunks festooned with waterlogged mosses. The air smelled of clean mountain rain and freshly dug earth. A green lizard, its nose shaped like a leaf, looked up at her from a low branch.

Now to get home and to Mother without being seen by Jansz and his men, who were probably still lurking around somewhere. Selvi was thankful that Amir hadn't told on her. He'd seemed nicer without his friends around, but she still had the uneasy feeling she shouldn't have told him about the men and Lokka the leopard.

Chapter Five

Selvi ran all the way home. She needed to get there before Jansz did. Her feet flew down the mountainside to the village below. Unlike Amir, who lived in the middle of nowhere, she lived in a hamlet made up of a dozen houses. This was how it was in this remote part of Serendib—a few hamlets scattered throughout the mountains, as well as remote, isolated dwellings tucked away among the peaks.

Selvi took her usual shortcut and squeezed through scraping branches onto the roof of her house, which was on a path lower than the wilderness behind. She dropped down to the ground at the front door and stood up, dusting her hands. She stepped back in fright when she noticed someone was there.

It was her uncle, Kandaraja, and he was staring at her in contempt.

Selvi groaned under her breath. Of all the bad luck! Why did he have to be visiting right now?

Just then, Jansz and one of his men came running around the corner. Uncle looked up at the noise and started when he saw who it was.

Selvi's heart was beating wildly. Uncle was bad enough on his own, always haranguing Mother about her parenting and Selvi's wildness. If the men started hassling Kandaraja about what happened on the mountainside, he'd come down even harder on her and she'd never be allowed out again.

She wanted to speak but didn't know what to say, how to explain the situation. But for some reason she couldn't understand, Jansz and his goon looked at each other and then took off. They disappeared down the path and around a bend, Jansz thumping heavily at the back.

Uncle turned to face Selvi. "Do you know those men?"

She shook her head silently. She wasn't sure if it was a lie, exactly, but she didn't really know anything about them. Other than the fact that they liked to kill harmless animals.

"Good. Stay away from them. They're good-for-nothings." Uncle Kandaraja smoothed down his immaculate full-white shirt and sarong.

Selvi's mother came to the door. "Brother," she said. "Sorry, were you waiting long? I was washing some clothes at the back and didn't hear you."

Uncle Kandaraja didn't answer but sighed, going past her into the house without invitation and settling himself down on the reed-woven chair.

Selvi followed him, dreading the conversation. Her uncle was her mother's much older brother. He was big on respectability, and what one should and shouldn't do, and keeping up appearances. Uncle was always interfering in their lives, and it annoyed Selvi that her mother always meekly listened and never stood up for herself.

"Get me something to drink, Gayathri," said Uncle. Mother went away at once to make him a hot drink.

Selvi bristled as she always did when he bossed them around. She turned to leave.

"Wait," said Uncle, snapping his fingers. "I haven't finished with you."

Uncle took his time, waiting for Mother to come back while Selvi stood there twiddling her thumbs and wondering what he had to say this time. She didn't dare leave, not because she was afraid of her uncle but because she didn't want to upset her mother.

Once Mother had handed her brother a cup, she perched nervously on the edge of a chair. Selvi stood there waiting. Uncle sipped slowly. Some small boys went past the open front door, rotating a wheel with a stick on the gravel outside and laughing noisily.

Uncle gestured to Selvi to take his cup once he'd finished. When she'd done so, he looked directly at Mother for the first time. Selvi hesitated on the way to the kitchen when she heard his words. "I was hoping that things would have improved around here. But nothing's changed. The girl still comes and goes whenever she wants."

Selvi's mother flushed. "She just likes being outdoors, brother. She's a little girl; I think it's good for her to be out playing."

"Playing?" roared Uncle suddenly, making them both jump. "Don't be ridiculous. She's twelve, not five. She should be home attending to her duties with you."

Selvi rolled her eyes inwardly as she put the cup down.

No one was sure what these duties were that Uncle kept going on about. She helped her mother with pounding the rice, and sometimes she cooked or helped with other things around the house. They grew some vegetables too. But she had time to go to school and do other things as well.

Mother nodded. "She does help—"

"Clearly not enough!" Uncle fiddled with the thick gold band on his wrist, which stood out against the dark brown of his skin. Uncle was very rich from his big shop in town, but his money created a problem for Selvi. He helped Mother financially, and in return he felt he could control everything about their lives.

He looked away suddenly, as if disgusted at the sight of them both, and stood up to go. "I will see you next week then. Although I'm sorry to see you're still not doing an adequate job of bringing the girl up properly."

Any brightness drained out of Mother's face at his parting shot. All his visits were like this. Short and abrupt, they always ended with her mother in tears and full of self-doubt. Uncle went out of the door and they watched him disappear down the path to where his cart would be waiting for him. Soon he'd be rolling off to his big house on a mountain peak.

"Good riddance!" Selvi turned to her mother. "Why do you put up with him?"

"Selvi!" Mother went back into the house wearily. "Don't talk about your uncle that way."

"I know you don't like this either!" Selvi followed her inside. "We don't need him. We get by just fine on the sewing that you do. Stop accepting his money."

Mother pressed a hand to her head. "He won't take no for an answer."

"Of course he won't! He wouldn't get to control our lives then."

"Okay, so he is a little strict—"

"Strict!" said Selvi. "This is beyond strict."

"Strict and old-fashioned then," said Mother placatingly. "A bit."

Selvi sighed. "No one thinks like him. Even his own family doesn't agree with him. I don't see why we have to listen."

"He cares about us, Selvi. He's been taking an interest in our lives ever since your father died. He could have left me to struggle alone but, as my older brother, he's thinking of his familial duty and is helping me." She scratched her hands in agitation, as she always did at the end of these visits. "He's probably right. I *am* too soft on you. It would be good for you to go out less and get ready for life."

"You're already preparing me for life! Whatever

that is. Stop listening to him." Selvi found the way her mother didn't stand up to Uncle so infuriating!

"Please, Selvi, that's enough. If I'm not doing a good enough job with you I'd rather know. My brother means well." She rubbed her temples and Selvi knew a headache must be coming on. "Go and get some water."

Selvi didn't want to agitate her any more so she went out of the back door to the well, picking up a basin from the kitchen on her way. This was a running argument between her and her mother. Her uncle had too much say in their lives, and it was always to Selvi's detriment. She *knew* Mother wasn't keen on the interference either, but she wanted to keep the peace and wouldn't ever challenge Uncle.

She dropped the bucket in the well and it hit the water with an echoing splash. Selvi pulled on the rope, cranking up the filled bucket the pulley. She placed the basin on the lip of the well and poured water into it. Picking up the basin, she turned to go.

She started and nearly dropped the basin, sloshing water down her skirt and feet.

Standing in front of her, in their little backyard, was Jansz.

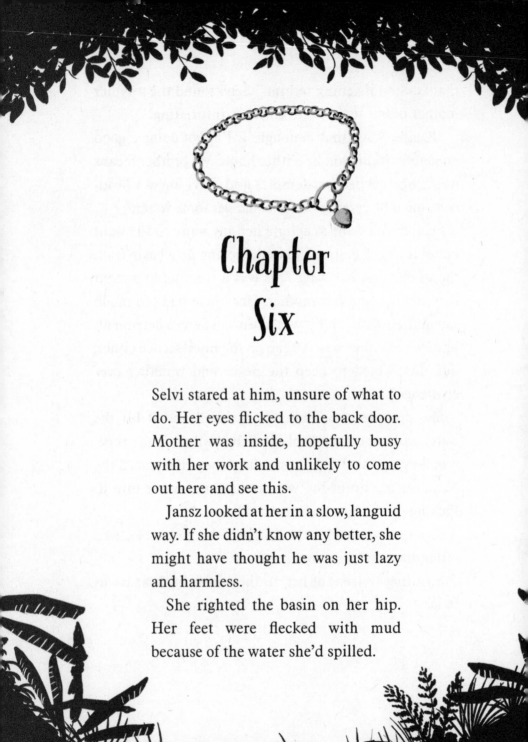

Chapter Six

Selvi stared at him, unsure of what to do. Her eyes flicked to the back door. Mother was inside, hopefully busy with her work and unlikely to come out here and see this.

Jansz looked at her in a slow, languid way. If she didn't know any better, she might have thought he was just lazy and harmless.

She righted the basin on her hip. Her feet were flecked with mud because of the water she'd spilled.

"Here," said Jansz, holding out something. "I think this is yours."

Without a word, Selvi held out her hand and he dropped her anklet into it.

"Look," he said, speaking heavily as if it was a lot of effort for the words to come out. "I don't want to hurt you."

Selvi decided to stay quiet so he'd keep talking. "We know that was you on the mountains."

Still she said nothing. He wasn't very bright. Obviously it was her. She'd admitted as much when she accepted the anklet.

"What you saw before," continued Jansz. "That was nothing, and none of your business. I want you to forget you saw anything."

She couldn't stay quiet anymore. "You can't go around killing leopards! There are laws—"

He held up a breadfruit-sized hand, talking over her. "Now, *if* you decided to tell someone . . ." He paused for his words to sink in.

Selvi shifted the basin on her hip. She couldn't let him threaten her into silence. There was no way she would let him kill Lokka, no matter what it took.

"It's just you and your mother at home, isn't it?" Jansz looked back toward the house and stroked his face as if thinking hard. "Wouldn't be very nice if something were to happen to her."

A cold fear clutched Selvi. No. Not Mother. She couldn't let anything—

"Leave my mother alone!" The words came out as a scream, and she had to work hard to stop the shaking in her voice. She took a deep breath and made a decision at once. "You have my word. I won't tell anyone."

Chapter Seven

Selvi ran down the mountain slope, her anklets jingling on her feet again. She looked over her shoulder and out of nowhere came a full-throated roar and a flash of rusty gold. A leopard came bounding after her, all power and muscle as he raced down the mountain. Soon enough, Lokka was running alongside Selvi in springing, bouncing leaps, their two figures making the only movement on the green mountainside.

They continued past gnarly rhododendron trees that reached to the sky, Selvi's feet slapping against the hard, uneven ground in tune with her jingling anklets. Her skirt flared around her, swishing over the soft purple nelu flowers that carpeted the mountainside. She flopped down and rolled partway while Lokka sprang out in one leap to the level below.

Selvi lay still for a moment and thought fleetingly that these flowers must have last shown themselves before she was born, as they only bloomed every twelve years. But Lokka was taking off again impatiently so she got up and sprinted after him.

Selvi came to a stop and doubled over, panting and laughing the way she always did when she ran with Lokka. She liked to pretend he was playing chase and hadn't been able to catch her, which was of course ridiculous because he could shoot past her in no time if he wanted to. Lokka stopped and waited. He knew the routine. He never came too close. But he enjoyed his daily run-around with Selvi before she set off for school and he retired, yawning, to his favorite spot to rest all day long.

"Bye, lazy!" she shouted, taking off for school. "See you later." She left him there to make his way back to the plateau and ran off.

She hurried all the way, going up and down another hill to the village school. The lightness of her morning left her as she came closer to the schoolhouse. The thought of seeing Amir again weighed heavily on her mind. Everything felt strange, as if the two parts of her world were colliding for the first time. Her steps were heavy as she entered the school compound.

The schoolhouse was open and airy, with a high, tiled roof and half-walls that made it seem as though they were outside. When it rained, Miss Heba rolled down the mats fixed on the sides so they wouldn't get wet. The children sat at rows of benches, all facing the front. Selvi made her way to her usual spot, in the third row on the left side, from where she could look out at the surrounding countryside. She put her bag down by her feet and tentatively looked around for Amir.

He was there already, messing around with a friend on the opposite side of the room. She smiled when she caught his eye. The friend whispered something to Amir, and they both burst out laughing. Selvi turned away angrily and slid farther into the end of her row, squashing herself against the rough wall marked with scribbles. Why, oh, why did she think that anything would be different just because of their encounter on the mountain? He was still the same Amir with the same stupid friends.

Within a few minutes, the noise became deafening as the room filled up with children. Everyone started settling into their places, although the bench Selvi sat at was the last to be occupied. There was a hush as Miss Heba mounted the steps and entered the school-room. She made her way to the front, the fall of her sari swishing elegantly behind her. Selvi liked Miss Heba. She wished she was as clever and as knowledgeable as her teacher.

Selvi hadn't been at the school for long. She'd been taught by Mother until a couple of months ago, at Uncle's insistence. But after a few years of trying, Miss Heba had finally persuaded Mother to send her to school, so she was there at last, much to Uncle's displeasure. It was an hour's walk from her home, and though Selvi enjoyed the lessons, she'd never connected with the other children. They thought she was strange and wild, and though she'd loved the idea of making some friends, they'd all spurned her.

A growling sound came from behind her and Selvi nearly jumped out of her skin. Children started looking around as another growl could be heard. Selvi turned around. It was coming from where Amir and his friends were sitting. They were all looking at her and shaking, trying hard not to laugh.

"Grr," said Amir's friend Ravindu, sending the others into more fits of silent laughter. Other kids started giggling and pointing, though not understanding what was going on. Amir blushed and looked away from Selvi.

She was furious with him. What had he *told* Ravindu?

Miss Heba put her bag down on her desk and sighed. "Amir, was that you?"

"No, miss," he said, standing up. He glanced slightly at Ravindu and smirked. "I think there's a leopard around here." He swayed to look under the bench, sending the children into peals of laughter.

"A leopard? I see." Miss Heba picked up a piece of chalk from the little box on her desk. "I don't like the beginning of our day to be disrupted. Or any part of the day, actually. So that leopard had better be quiet. If I hear it *once more*, Amir, I'll be sending you home."

"*Me?* But, miss—"

"That'll be all, Amir. If I send you home I will need to see your mother tomorrow for a chat."

With that Amir sat down, glowering, and stayed quiet for the rest of the day. At home time, Selvi packed up her things quickly. That way, she could leave at the same time as the teacher and not be left with the others, thus avoiding Amir and his silly friends. She felt foolish for thinking that he'd have changed after their one interaction, and she couldn't bear to stay there a minute longer than necessary.

Unfortunately, a group of girls deliberately formed a huddle in front of her, blocking the way out of her row. The sound of their chattering made her want to scream. Miss Heba went down the steps into the sun, shifting her bag on to her shoulder for the walk home. "Grr," said one of the girls, making the others burst out laughing. At least Amir had the decency to look embarrassed. Nobody knew what this was really about, but everyone wanted to get in on it.

Selvi pushed her way through the throng of girls and out into the yard. She raced away from their taunting voices, initially heading toward home but then turning up the path toward Lokka's mountain hangout instead. She hurried past the mist of a towering waterfall, eager to get away from the school and check on the leopard to make sure he was all right. She had to think of a way to move him somehow so that Jansz couldn't find him. She stopped for a moment and pricked ears. She could hear something faintly over the sound of her anklets and the gush of the waterfall behind her. A rustling, panting noise that stopped every time she did. It wasn't Lokka, of course. He was sure-footed and moved about effortlessly, whereas this was clumsier and altogether more human.

Selvi had a good idea who it could be.

She ran her hand over the rock in front of her, pretending to examine something on it. A bush behind her swished, and she turned around quickly to see a face disappearing back into the foliage.

Selvi pounced and dragged Amir out. He struggled and lashed out at her, taken by surprise. "What are you *doing?*"

"What are *you* doing?" Selvi asked angrily, rubbing at her scratched forearms. "Stop following me!"

"I'm not!" he said, looking outraged. "I just want to see the leopard."

"What?!" Selvi was startled. A thought dawned on her. "Did you . . . Did you see me this morning?"

"Only from afar," he said, biting his lip as if he were reluctant to admit it. "I was near the top of the waterfall."

"So you were spying on me?" she said icily.

He carried on chewing his lip. "There's a rumor that you're friendly with leopards and that's why you spend all your time in the mountains." He paused, as if embarrassed. "People say that you can speak to them. I wanted to see if it's true."

"Of course it's not true!" She was starting to realize why the children thought she was strange. Although if it were true, it would be marvelous! "I *wish* I could talk to leopards but I can't."

"How did you do that this morning then?"

"Do what?" Selvi strode off, stamping her feet on the ground in annoyance, but he followed her. How dare he snoop on her and then want explanations!

"Running around with the leopard," persisted Amir, hurrying alongside her. "You weren't scared of it. How come it didn't run away? Or try to kill you?"

Selvi was seething. Now she knew what the leopard noises had been about!

"Why should I tell you anything?" She ducked under a low-hanging semina tree.

Amir came around from the other side, popping up in front of her. "Why shouldn't you? I helped you, didn't I? I didn't tell Jansz where you were."

"That doesn't matter," she said, pushing past him and stomping up the path. "I'm not afraid of him anymore." She didn't mention that the reason she wasn't afraid was because she'd agreed to his terms.

"I still did it, didn't I? I just want to *see*. Please! How did you control the leopard like that?"

"Control?" Selvi stopped, confused. "Lokka is a wild animal. I do not *control* him."

"It has a name!"

"Of course he has a name. Why wouldn't he?"

Amir looked excited. "I can't believe it. Does it respond to you calling its name? Are you able to tell it to do stuff?"

Selvi was chilled by his words and felt uneasy.

Lokka wasn't some sort of plaything.

"No," she said shortly. "I'm not able to do any of that."

But Amir wouldn't give up. "How was it running after you then? Sort of . . . playing. I mean, it didn't try to attack you or anything, like it would have done anyone else. Normally it's so difficult to even spot them, as they run away." He prattled on, super excited.

"Wait a minute," she said. "Did you *tell* anyone what you saw?"

Amir tore off a clump of leaves from a nearby tree and stuffed it in his mouth, as if to stop the words coming out. Totally shifty behavior, Selvi thought. "Only my friend Ravindu," he said, his words muffled by the disgusting mess of chewed leaves in his mouth.

"What?! You had no right!"

Amir had told Ravindu about Lokka. Selvi had never told *anyone* about him. Not a soul. Now the whole class knew, or would know soon. She was trying to *hide* the leopard because of Jansz, not have loads of more people looking for him.

"Why would I show you anything?" she said. "Yes, you helped me, but you couldn't keep that a secret, could you? Lokka's in *huge* danger already. I don't want more people finding out about him."

"Ravindu doesn't know I'm here. And he's a friend; nothing bad is going to happen. Look, I'm not going to do anything, I just want to *see*."

"There's nothing *to* see." Selvi stamped her foot. "I have to go home now," she said. She wasn't going to take Amir to Lokka. "My mother is waiting for me."

"I thought your house was that way," said Amir, pointing in the opposite direction helpfully.

"I know where my house is. Just leave me alone. Did you tell Ravindu about Jansz?"

"Jansz?" Amir's brow furrowed for a moment. "Oh, I get it. That's the man who was looking for you. No, I didn't mention him."

"Good! Keep it that way! I can't have anybody know about him." As soon as the words were out, she knew she'd said too much. She could have kicked herself.

Amir's eyes narrowed, as if he were thinking hard. "So I shouldn't tell anyone that you saw Jansz shoot the leopard? Fine, I'll keep your secret. But in return, take me to your leopard."

Chapter Eight

Selvi's head throbbed in frustration.

"I told you," said Amir. "I won't tell anyone about this. I just want to see the leopard. Please."

Selvi was furious at being put in such a position. The *last* thing she wanted to do was involve Amir with Lokka. But what if he told someone? Jansz would think that she'd broken her end of the deal and his gang would come after her and Mother. If she made an enemy of Amir, she would be putting herself and Mother in danger.

"That's blackmail," said Selvi.

Amir frowned. "I don't even know what that is."

"It means you're forcing me to do something because you have information you could reveal."

"Well, that sounds bad," he said, "but I'm not forcing you to do anything. I'm *pleading* with you."

She took a deep breath. He sounded more clueless than sneaky. Maybe he didn't mean any harm. "Okay, you win," she said. "You can come."

Selvi set off up the mountain again, hoping against hope that they wouldn't find Lokka. Amir followed behind. She moved slowly, willing Lokka to be away from his favorite spot. What would she do if he was there? She hoped he'd run away at the sight of Amir.

"I don't know how you do it!" said Amir enthusiastically as they jumped over a dip in the ground. "Such a big leopard. And it was just playing with you like a cat."

Selvi glanced at him. Amir was gesturing and smiling, his face full of happiness. She had to admit, his enthusiasm was infectious. It made her smile a little in spite of her irritation with him. She'd never had anyone to talk to about Lokka and the bond she shared with him, and it was tempting to trust Amir. She thought back to yesterday when they were at his house. He'd seemed nice. Yes, he'd acted like an idiot with his friends that morning in school, but when it came to it, he hadn't betrayed her. She decided to give him another chance.

"It didn't happen right away," she said. "At first I think Lokka was curious. He'd seen me on the mountains a lot. And for some reason I wasn't afraid of him. I caught glimpses of him now and then but I just kept out of his way. But then he began to watch me. After a long time of doing that, he came over. I was terrified!"

Amir's eyes grew wider and wider in surprise until he resembled a loris. "No way! What did you do?"

"Nothing." Selvi laughed. "I just stood there frozen to the spot. He had a good look and then ran off. The next time it happened, I was less scared. And after it happened a few times, I wasn't afraid of him. So he just kept staying longer and longer."

"That's like . . . the best thing ever." Amir looked almost reverential with wonder.

Selvi smiled. "It's quite special."

"Why don't you go near him then?" said Amir as they neared the plateau that was Lokka's favorite haunt. "You said you don't get close."

"I don't know really." She hadn't actually thought about it. "It just feels like the right thing to do. He's a wild animal, so though we have this bond, I want to keep a respectful distance."

"How do you know where to find him?" he said, brushing aside a low branch as they trudged upward.

"I don't. It's not like I necessarily know where he is at any time. But he has a favorite spot. Do you know the small plateau high up in the mountains there," she said, pointing, "which the villagers call the 'small end-of-the-world'? He likes to hang out there."

"Yes! I can't believe I'll get to see him. Do you think he'll like me too?"

"Maybe," said Selvi. "Either that or he'll eat you. We'll soon find out." She giggled at the startled look on Amir's face until he realized she was joking.

Eventually they came to the high point on which Lokka would normally be found. It was a flat area of sandy, rocky ground, ringed with wilderness on three sides and a plunging drop on the fourth.

Sure enough, there was Lokka, his spotted body nestled languidly in his favorite tree as if he didn't have a care in the world. The setting sun blazed through him, silhouetting him and his hanging tail. He turned slowly as Selvi approached. Amir stopped abruptly behind her.

Selvi stood back and grinned at him. Lokka yawned, his mouth open wide and revealing four long, curving canines and smaller jagged teeth behind them. A pink, bristled tongue stretched out. He flicked his tail in greeting. He was absolutely perfect.

"Whoa," whispered Amir. "Whoa. Whoa. Whoa." Each word was punctuated by silence.

Selvi chuckled at his reaction. He stood there gaping, his gaze creeping left and right at the plateau, but always coming back to the resting leopard in the tree.

Lokka rolled his head and looked at Amir briefly, then settled back again.

Amir looked as if he desperately wanted to get closer, but he hung back. It was probably for the best. Selvi wasn't sure how Lokka would react to a stranger, though he didn't seem overly concerned as he lay there in the golden light.

"Let's go back," said Selvi. She didn't want to stay too long with Amir there.

"What? That's it? You're not going to run around with him?" He looked behind reluctantly as they walked off.

"No. He's always like this at this time of day. He's more active in the morning, maybe after a night of prowling and hunting."

Amir's mouth turned down at the corners in disappointment, but he brightened up soon and started on the questions again. "How do you always know it's him? All leopards look more or less the same."

"No, they don't. They are as varied as humans. And this area is his territory anyway. Also, haven't you noticed his coat? He has a golden shimmer around his rosettes."

"Oh yes. How come it's like that?"

"I don't know. I've never seen anything like it."

He turned back to look but they'd left Lokka high up behind them as they descended the mountain. Amir seemed reluctant for his adventure to be over. "What are you going to do about those men?"

"I need to convince Lokka to leave. He's not safe here now. Maybe once Jansz has given up, Lokka can come back. This is his territory, after all, and he shouldn't be chased away by those idiots."

"Why do they want him?" asked Amir.

Selvi frowned at him. "Isn't it obvious? His skin!" she said impatiently. "Bones, teeth."

Amir looked revolted. "What? Bones and teeth? Why?"

"There are parts of the world where big-cat skins are used as rugs. Or bags and other stupid things. Bones and teeth are used in some types of medicine. I've heard that people like Jansz take the animals to the port and sell them to the foreign merchants as the ships arrive."

They'd come to the track that led to Amir's house. They stopped there for a moment before Selvi turned to be on her way.

"Wait a minute. Does this mean," said Amir, "that if Jansz gets your leopard . . ."

Selvi grimaced. "I've got to go. I promised my mother I'd help with the rice."

Her heart burned as she continued down the path toward home. Amir's unfinished sentence hung in the air, blurring the fern-covered path ahead of her as tears stung her eyes. He was right, of course. She couldn't bear to think about it, but if Jansz got to him, Lokka could end up as a rug on somebody's floor.

Chapter Nine

The next day Selvi was late for school. She ran all the way down to the schoolhouse, hoping that she wouldn't get into trouble with Miss Heba. She and Mother had been winnowing till late the previous evening, separating the rice from the husk on woven fan-trays. Her neck and arms were aching but the good thing was that they now had a nice cleaned batch of rice that would last them three months at least.

Miss Heba was in the middle of a lesson when she arrived and waved her away without a word. All the mean kids from Amir's side of the room looked up at her. Amir smiled. Ravindu looked at him quizzically. Amir quickly wiped the smile off his face and ducked his head. Selvi went hurriedly to her usual row.

The room was stuffy today. Selvi didn't have her end seat so she had to sit on the aisle, and she could hear Ravindu whispering. She glanced at Amir, bent over his bench, but he didn't look back. Ravindu had something in his palm that he was showing Amir. Selvi leaned back slightly and caught the glint of a shiny copper coin. Amir glanced at it briefly but then he kept his eyes down. The whispering from Ravindu continued.

"What's going on?" Miss Heba sighed. One of the littlest children in the front row stood up with her slate in her hand to see what the teacher was looking at. "Ravindu, Amir?"

"Nothing, miss," said Ravindu, smirking at Selvi. Amir ignored the whole thing, as if pretending not to be there.

Selvi glared at Amir, even though he wasn't looking at her. She just couldn't figure him out. Why did he always act so strangely when his friends were around? When school had finished, a group of children surrounded Ravindu and Amir in the front yard. They were talking excitedly, with Ravindu showing them the coin Selvi had seen earlier. Selvi gathered that they were going down to town to buy something, but she rushed past them without stopping. Mother had asked her to come straight home after school as they were going to visit Uncle. But Selvi hadn't been able to see Lokka that morning so she felt she had to go and check on him.

Just a quick look at Lokka and I'll be away, she told herself as she ran up the path, leaving the chatter of the excited children behind her.

"Hey!" said Amir, coming up behind her, panting. His cheeks were red as if he'd been running hard to catch up. "Wait for me. Are you going to see your leopard?"

Selvi rolled her eyes at him. "Is it my imagination, or do you only talk to me when you want something?" she said.

He blushed and looked ashamed. "It isn't that. We just have different friends in school . . ." He stopped, probably realizing how pathetic that sounded.

"It's okay, you don't have to make excuses," she said. She didn't understand it and she wasn't interested in hearing explanations for his behavior. She had bigger things to worry about. "Aren't you going to town though? I thought your friends were leaving."

Amir twiddled his thumbs. "I . . . er, I'd prefer to see the leopard. If you'll have me."

"You can come if you want." Selvi shrugged.

Amir smiled in gratitude, and they carried on up the mountainside.

The ground was slippery with dew so they stayed on the path and didn't try to find a shortcut up the rocky face of the mountain. A sambar deer walked on the slopes, its thick, curving antlers picked out in the sapphire afternoon sky.

Eventually they came to Lokka's plateau. Selvi, climbing ahead of Amir, suddenly stopped and pulled him behind a tree.

A man was pacing back and forth on Lokka's plateau. It was Jansz.

"He *said* the leopard would be here!" He was talking to one of his men, who was sitting on a rock nearby.

Selvi turned to Amir in stunned silence. Jansz had found Lokka's plateau already! Amir stared back, looking ashen with fear.

"It's been ages," said the man. "We should move on and track him down."

"We need to lay some traps, Liyanage," said Jansz. "Put down poisoned meat if we have to." He suddenly roared, making Selvi jump. "We need to get this leopard! We HAVE to find it by next Thursday."

Selvi could hardly believe what she was hearing. Her

ears rang at his words. *Traps? Poison?* What chance would Lokka have against these things? Her hands tightened around the branch she was hiding behind as she stared with hatred at Jansz. Amir had closed his eyes and his forehead rested against the trunk.

"That only gives us eight days," said Liyanage. "Why Thursday?"

"The boss has a buyer waiting at the port, but he's leaving soon." Jansz kicked a bush as if Lokka was going to be under it. "Thursday's our last chance to sell it."

"Let's forget this leopard," said Liyanage sulkily. "We've been trying so long. There are others just as good."

"Don't be stupid." Jansz looked at the man in contempt. "This is the best specimen we've ever seen. The boss said it has to be this one. Do you want to tell him we didn't get it?"

That shut up Liyanage. "Let's wait and see if it shows up then."

Jansz stopped pacing. "No, you're right. We should check the forest on the other hill. We'll come back here tomorrow if it's not there. Put down some snares."

Selvi and Amir watched silently as the men made their way from the plateau. They saw them appear at various points down the hill until they disappeared into a thicket and were gone.

Selvi turned to the boy, who was looking at her fearfully. "Did you hear that?" she whispered. "They mean to kill Lokka. And they mean to kill him in whatever way it takes." She moved away from Amir and put her head in her hands. "How can I stop him falling into a trap?" she cried. "Or eating meat that might be poisoned?"

Amir swallowed. "I'm sorry," he said. "But we can try to make him leave. Before they . . . do those things. Then they'll be forced to give up and look for another cat."

But she shook her head in despair. "I don't want a different leopard to be killed either. But you heard them! They don't just want any old leopard by next week. They want *Lokka*."

Chapter
Ten

The next day, for some reason Selvi couldn't understand, Ravindu spoke to her at school. She'd just settled into her seat and the teacher wasn't there yet. Children were still coming in, slapping their bags and lunches on the benches and talking noisily.

"Hey, Selvi," said Ravindu, shouting across the class from where he was sitting. "We're going fishing after school. Do you want to come?"

Selvi was too surprised to answer

at first. She wasn't sure what had come over the boy. She looked for Amir and was surprised to see that he wasn't in his usual place. She thought he hadn't come in at first, but then she spotted him in the back row. He had his head buried in his bag as if he were looking for something.

Selvi sighed. "No," she said to Ravindu shortly. She turned away and looked out of the window, not wanting to engage with whatever he was playing at.

"Oh, come on!" said Ravindu. "It'll be fun. Amir said you'd enjoy it."

Selvi looked back to see Amir jerk his head out of his bag and glare at Ravindu. When he saw Selvi looking his way he dived into his bag again.

"I'll come!" said a girl next to Selvi, taking out a crumpled lunch pack from an extremely tattered bag.

But Ravindu made a face and turned away, clearly not interested in her. The girl, Minoli, huffed and muttered something at him under her breath.

Selvi ignored them for the rest of the day, but she wondered what was up with Amir and Ravindu. When Miss Heba was talking to Salma, a tiny girl in the front row who'd brought her kitten to school, she leaned over to Minoli next to her and whispered, "Why is Amir sitting apart from Ravindu?"

Minoli stared at her in astonishment. Selvi couldn't blame her; she'd never taken an interest in any kind of classroom gossip. To her relief, though, Minoli was happy to oblige and lowered her voice conspiratorially. "They had a *big* argument before school in the play-ground. No one knows about what. They were about to start beating each other up but a passing farmer separated them."

Selvi was startled. "I didn't think Amir was the fighting type," she whispered.

"He isn't. That's why everyone's surprised." Minoli spread out her hands. "Who knows?"

"Didn't they say anything?" She leaned in closer to Minoli. "No clues at all?"

"There was something about the coin Ravindu had yesterday. He wouldn't say how he got it, but Ravindu swears he didn't steal it and that it was given to him. Amir seemed mad about it." She shrugged and screwed up her face in confusion.

"Oh. But wh—"

"Selvi!" said Miss Heba, staring at her from the front. Even though she seemed ready to tell Selvi off, she looked a bit reluctant. It was the first time Selvi had had a conversation with anyone in the class. "You two can talk some other time. Now it's time for learning, okay?"

Selvi nodded, and Miss Heba went back to talking about soil types. There was a deep feeling of unease in Selvi. She looked over at Amir in the back row. He was staring into space with a look of intense misery on his face. It was the same expression he'd had yesterday when they'd seen Jansz up on Lokka's plateau.

The sound of chalk clacking on the board and Miss Heba's voice drew her attention back to the front. But Selvi couldn't concentrate. How did Jansz know exactly where to look for Lokka? Other than her, only Amir knew about it.

He *wouldn't*. Would he?

As soon as Miss Heba dismissed them, Selvi ran off to Lokka's plateau. The day was dry and sunny and she left the path and went back to scaling the mountains again. It felt good to feel the hot rock under her feet and hands. Two giant dandu squirrels came bouncing down a keena tree, twitching this way and that and frolicking on the grass. At the top of the hill, Selvi ran over to the plateau. She was wearing her anklets again, so if Lokka were there, he'd know she was approaching without being surprised.

She kept an eye out for Jansz and his men as she raced up. She had to be super careful. How much did he know?

Lokka wasn't in the tree this time. He was sitting in his other favorite place, the flat sandy ground in front of the ledge. He was lazing around as usual. As she got closer he flipped on to his back and rubbed his body on the ground, white sand flying in the air. Then he rolled back to his stomach and was still again, yawning and watching Selvi closely.

Selvi kept her distance and sat on a bench-shaped rock on the side, drawing her feet up. She was sickened by how close the net was closing around Lokka. Was he even aware of the danger he was in?

Lokka looked directly at the girl. He blinked in that way he always did, a super-quick movement where he screwed up his eyes and opened them again. His gaze seemed to be probing her, as the amber irises and dark flecks on the outer edges of his eyes made him look both peaceful and mysterious. What she would give to know what he was thinking!

"Lokka, you have to listen to me," said Selvi. Although she felt that they understood each other, she didn't usually talk to him. They generally went about their day together in companionable silence or with her screaming in exhilaration. "You're not safe here. Those men who shot an arrow at you, they mean to get you. And get you soon. This place is dangerous and you must leave."

Lokka stared back at her evenly.

Selvi looked away in frustration. How could she make him understand? This was his territory. He wouldn't leave it without good reason. But she couldn't protect him from Jansz and his men. They might be laying traps all over the place at that very moment.

Selvi felt so alone. Briefly, in the beginning, she'd thought that Amir might help. But she couldn't trust him to understand how serious things were. Instead of keeping her secret, he'd actually managed to increase the number of people who knew about the leopard.

Then, without warning, Lokka stood up and stared at her even more intently. He took a few steps toward her and then stopped again.

"What's the matter?" Selvi said, confused. He seemed more watchful than aggressive, but he'd never come toward her like that before.

Suddenly he crouched low. He stalked toward her, head lowered and shoulders hunched, taking quick, measured strides.

The hairs on the back of Selvi's neck stood up. Surely not. He wouldn't . . . He was a friend! They knew each other well. He'd never attack her.

Would he?

Lokka continued to creep toward her, silent and stealthy, a deadly look in his eyes.

Selvi shrank back and covered her head with her crossed arms.

Then, his huge claws unsheathed, Lokka sprang.

Chapter Eleven

Lokka landed smoothly on the rock next to Selvi, before bounding away again in one graceful movement.

Selvi's heart raced as she turned around to see the leopard running so fast he was almost a blur. He sprang at a spotted deer, which had been grazing peacefully on the mountain-side, before sinking his jaws into the animal's neck. The deer went down and there was a brief struggle in the tall grass.

Selvi turned away and covered her ears. She'd witnessed this once before and had no wish to do so again. Lokka walked back to the plateau a few minutes later, dragging the deer's carcass in his mouth. He proceeded to climb his tree swiftly, settling his lunch in the branches.

"Did you see that?" shouted Amir, coming out of nowhere and startling Selvi. "I saw the whole thing!"

"Well, I was sitting right here," said Selvi crossly.

Amir, stalking her again. She was never sure when he was going to pop up behind her. She turned away and tried to tune out the sound of Lokka noisily tearing into his meal.

Amir was, of course, completely oblivious to her annoyance. "Why does he eat up in the tree?" he asked, looking on with interest.

"It's to protect his food from other animals who might want a piece," she said curtly.

"But isn't he like . . . the animal that no one else eats?"

"Yes, he's the top predator in Serendib. But there are other animals like jackals that would want some of his prey."

"This place!" said Amir, leaving Lokka to his food and walking to the flat ridge that overlooked the scenery below. "I can't believe it. It really *is* like standing on the edge of the world." He stood there and gaped at the scene in front of him. The thick wilderness covered the mountains and there was an endless expanse of light-blue sky above. To the west and slightly below the plateau, a waterfall descended, its never-ending cascade silent at this distance. Below them was a dizzying drop into misty nothingness.

"Hey, don't get too close to the edge," called out Selvi.

Amir didn't need to be told twice and whipped back to Selvi, his mind on Lokka once again. "That poor deer didn't stand a chance! The leopard was so fast! Did you see how he sprang through the air?" He made a flying motion with one hand and smacked it against the other. "Have you seen that before?"

"Well, I once saw him attack a buffalo." Selvi shuddered at the memory. "It was twice his size."

"What happened?"

"The buffalo put up a good fight. I didn't stay to watch. I think Lokka had to retreat that time, maybe. The next time I saw him he had a cut under one eye and lots of scratches."

Selvi was getting more and more incensed with Amir while they talked, but she wanted to give him a chance to explain himself. She saw Lokka jump down from the tree and walk lazily to the edge of the plateau. His gait was measured and slow, probably because of his full stomach, and his long tail trailed on the ground. He settled himself where Amir had just been standing and looked out over the horizon at the vast drop and his kingdom of mountain wilderness below.

"Ha! It kind of serves him right," said Amir. "For trying to kill a buffalo."

Selvi shrugged. "That's just food for him. It's how he survives."

Lokka flicked his tail over his coat, the golden hue on it shimmering in soft rings. In this light he looked like a mythical creature. Selvi couldn't help but marvel at his majesty.

Then Amir spoke and the spell was broken. "Selvi?" Amir said hesitantly. "I've been thinking. You know what we should do next?"

She couldn't bear it any longer, now that he was trying to make plans with her. "*We? We* are not going to be doing anything! Some friend you are."

He stopped and stared at her. "What's come over you?"

"I *know*, Amir." She stood up from the rock and walked over to him. She stabbed the air with a finger. "I know it was your pal Ravindu who told Jansz."

Amir stood there motionless, a horrified look on his face. A cold breeze blew down through the mountains and flapped his hair about. "Selvi, I . . . It's not how it looks."

"I *trusted* you. *Why*, I don't know!" She threw up her hands and shook her head in disbelief. "But you betrayed me, and you betrayed Lokka."

"I'm sorry." Amir was distraught. "I don't know why I did it. It's just, the leopard. The running. All of this . . ." He waved his arm about. "Everything was so amazing. I just had to—"

"You had to show off," she finished. "You couldn't keep your mouth shut, you had to tell Ravindu, and now everything's ruined."

Amir began to pace the area in agitation. "I didn't think he'd speak to Jansz! It was meant to be a secret. All I told him was that you had this bond with the leopard and that—" He paused and looked away shamefacedly. "And that I was going to learn to make him do things too."

"You don't get it, do you! It's not about making him *do* anything. I don't control him!" She looked down the mountainside, her frustration with Amir growing by the second. "Why did Ravindu tell Jansz anyway?"

"I don't know," he said tearfully. "Ravindu had been sneaking around here trying to spot the leopard when he came across Jansz. They talked and Ravindu told him about you and how you are with the leopard. Jansz gave him money and promised more if he helped catch Lokka."

"Well, that's just *great!* You've only gone and made it nice and easy for him."

So Jansz now knew about her connection to Lokka. Amir couldn't have made things any worse if he'd tried.

"I'm so sorry, Selvi. I really am. I made a huge mistake and I've been so angry at myself, and at Ravindu for making this worse. But I want to help fix things. Please let me."

Lokka growled from his position at the edge of the plateau. He clearly wanted to spend his afternoon in peace, not have children squabbling in his territory.

Selvi stepped away. It wasn't fair, she realized. They'd better leave him in peace. "No way," she said to Amir, shaking her finger at him. "I'll figure out things on my own. It's always been that way, and it's always what's worked for me."

Amir's face clouded over at the slight. "All right then," he said, his eyes misting up. "If that's what you want. I messed up, and I get why you're mad."

He sniffed and wiped his face with a grubby hand, leaving dirty streaks on his cheeks. He backed away from her. "I'll just go—"

"AMIR! NO!" Selvi froze as Amir stepped back onto Lokka's tail. The huge leopard sprang up with a roar and Amir teetered wildly. Selvi raced over to them.

Lokka reared up on to his back legs and swiped at Amir, making the boy scream in terror. Selvi reached out and Amir grabbed her hard, clinging on for dear life.

Selvi yelled as she lost her balance and fell forward, knocking into Lokka. The three of them wobbled together on the edge of the plateau for a heart-stopping moment, then plunged over the precipice.

Chapter Twelve

Selvi's arms flailed as she fell, and her hand found a creeper growing in the rock. She grabbed it but it broke away and she fell farther, Amir clinging to her. She hit the side of the mountain and managed to grasp a clump of vines with both hands. Her feet found a narrow ledge and she gripped it with her toes. Amir clung to her like a dead weight, pulling her down. Next to his feet, Lokka struggled for a grip on the ledge, his claws scraping madly on the rock.

"Amir! You've got to let go of me," said Selvi. "Quick! You're weighing us both down and I can't hold on."

Amir whimpered. His eyes were closed. Lokka growled but Amir seemed not to notice. He kept his eyes shut and moaned under his breath.

"Listen to me, Amir." Selvi spoke firmly and authoritatively. All she wanted to do was shake him and tell him to get a hold of himself, but they were hanging on for their lives on the side of a huge cliff so that wasn't a good idea at all. "I want you to take a deep breath, open your eyes and only look at what's in front of you."

Amir didn't react. Lokka scrabbled at the rock. He was clinging on by his front paws to the ledge and looked okay for the moment, but they'd fallen too far for him to leap back on to the plateau. He was practically vertical, using his back legs and tail to anchor himself to the rock.

"Amir! Listen to me!" said Selvi forcefully. The vine in her right hand came away and she clawed at another one. A chill breeze swept over them, flattening the tufts of grass on the rocks and making her arms break out in goosebumps.

Below them was nothing. Selvi looked away as a wave of dizziness passed over her. She wasn't afraid of heights, but this was a new level of dangerous for her.

Amir opened his eyes reluctantly. He stared at the rock in front of him. "Are we dead?" he said, his voice small and crushed.

"No, but we will be soon if you don't *take your hands off me.*" Her arms were straining and she had bloody scrapes all over her body. Her knees stung from where they'd grazed the rock.

Amir shifted slightly and looked down. "No, don't!"

Too late. His face crumpled.

He whimpered again and shut his eyes. "I can't do this, Selvi. We're going to die. We're going to die."

"No, we're not. Look, let's do this one step at a time." She had to keep talking. Keep making him not think of the fact that they were clinging to the side of a cliff wall and could plunge to certain death at any minute.

Amir didn't respond at all, just kept his eyes shut and whispered something under his breath. Selvi could make out the sound of prayers.

"Amir," she said. "Listen to me. We can give up and die. Or we can try to help ourselves and have a chance of surviving." Though his eyes were closed, she could tell from his face that he was thinking. Selvi felt panic at the time that was passing and the numbness that was spreading through her arms. They were a trio of ants clinging to a vertical drop and they couldn't hold on forever.

"Okay," he said in a small voice. He was sweating profusely in spite of the chill. But at least he was responding.

"Now listen to me. You don't realize it, but you're standing on a little ledge. I am too. I want you to feel around with your feet and get yourself into the best position, one where you feel safest, and then take one hand off me." Selvi pointed at something with her nose. "See that vine there? Hold on to that."

He looked at it, terrified. "But that's not going to hold me up!"

"We don't have a lot of choice here, Amir. You'll be okay. Trust me, that's actually a good, strong vine."

Amir loosened his hand from her upper arm and Selvi gasped as the blood began to circulate through it again.

"Hurry up!" said Selvi. "We haven't got all day." He reached out and grasped the vine.

"Well done. Now, try to think like an animal and transfer your weight equally to all four limbs." She wondered if she was confusing him but she didn't know how else to explain it. Slowly, he did as she said and she felt his weight lift off her.

To her relief, Amir seemed to be doing all right. The blood had drained from his face and he was shaking, but he clung on determinedly. He gazed at the rock in front of him as if fascinated by it. She was glad that his mind was fully focused.

"I'm really proud of you, Amir," said Selvi. "You're doing great."

Selvi looked to the rock above them. She knew she had to climb back up to the plateau and get help. She'd never climbed anything quite like *this*, but if anyone could do it, she knew it was her.

"What do we do now?" asked Amir, just as Lokka, who was starting to struggle, gave a growl.

Amir hadn't realized Lokka was right there with them and, startled, he gave a scream. In his shock, he let go of the vine.

Chapter Thirteen

Before she had time to think, Selvi swung out and grabbed Amir with one hand. She hung on wildly as he dangled in the air, before he came to his senses and grasped a clump of thiththa leaves and pulled himself back toward the ledge. He found his footing again and sidled toward Selvi. "What are you doing!" she said, her fear making her furious.

"Lokka's right there!" said Amir in a high-pitched voice.

"Of course he is! You pulled him down, remember? Right after you stepped on his tail."

"I didn't know he was there," said Amir tearfully. "And now he's too close. He's angry with me."

"No, he isn't. He was annoyed with you. He has bigger things to concern him now."

"But—but . . ." Amir seemed to be losing his nerve again. "He's a wild animal. What about that thing about keeping a respectful distance?"

She sighed. "What do you think he can do to you here?"

Amir glared at her. "A leopard never changes its spots."

In spite of everything, Selvi snorted. Amir looked angrily at her, making her chuckle even more.

"Sorry," she said. "Look, just hold on. I'm going to climb back up to the plateau and get help."

"*WHAT?*"

"Well, we can't just hang about here all day."

"Climb up there?" Amir looked fearful again, his voice was pleading. "Don't do it, Selvi. I can't stay here alone. You'll die and I'll be left here with the leopard."

"Thanks for the vote of confidence. But I'm doing it. All you have to do is hold on and be safe. And whatever you do, *don't look down*." Despite her casual tone, Selvi was tight with nerves. One wrong move and she'd be smashed to smithereens. *Deep breath,* she told herself. *Look ahead and upward only.* Selvi began to move and immediately disturbed a cluster of relict ants that scattered across the rock.

Suddenly Selvi didn't feel afraid anymore. She was in her element. Climbing came as naturally as walking to her. *Jingle, jingle, jingle* went the bells on her anklets. Her feet found crevices and protrusions to grip on to, sometimes twisting sideways from her body to get into the best positions to hold her. She was small and light, but she'd learned to make herself even lighter, spreading her weight to all four limbs as she'd told Amir to. She knew which rock foliage was the best for holding on to. It wasn't necessarily always the strongest-looking either. Those actually broke more easily. A handful of the thin and wiry plants was much better.

She gripped a reed and twisted it around her palms before pulling herself higher. She wondered for a moment if Amir would lose his nerve and grab at her feet, but he didn't, and she climbed on. Slowly, slowly, one rock-hold at a time, the top of the cliff came closer, Selvi's breath catching with every glimpse of the matted greenery at the top. Soon she was close enough to see drops of moisture on the grass.

The lip of the cliff was the hardest part. It was also the most dangerous, and where all her hard work could be undone.

Her fingers found the top and she braced herself for going over. Slowly, she pulled herself upward. She had to be spiderlike here, using a leg first to anchor herself instead of trying to hoist her whole weight on her forearms. She was soon halfway over the top, with one leg over it, insect-like. Her head lifted over the cliff, and the flatland there was the most welcome sight in the world. She gave one last huge effort and rolled over the lip on to the flat ground. She collapsed there and lay for a few minutes, catching her breath.

A whimper from below made her crawl to the edge and look down, flat on her stomach.

"Forgotten me, Selvi?" called out Amir. His voice was pleading.

"Never," she said. She paused, then craned farther out for a better view. Her blood ran cold.

"Amir," she said, trying to keep her voice calm. "Where is Lokka?"

Amir turned his head stiffly, trying to look along the ledge. There was nothing there. Where previously Lokka had been hanging and clawing at the ledge he was standing on, it was now empty. Even from this distance Selvi could see the claw marks on the rock.

"I . . . I don't know," he said.

"I know he didn't come up," she whispered, hardly able to articulate the words. "Or I'd have seen him."

"But he didn't fall down," said Amir. "I know he didn't. He would have roared, or struggled, or something."

"So where is he then?"

Amir looked helplessly at her and shook his head. "I really don't know."

"Where are you, Lokka?" she whispered. Tears started to fall down her face and drip on the ground. She'd lost him. Her friend, her silent companion, the leopard she'd tried so hard to save, had disappeared into thin air.

Chapter Fourteen

Selvi put her head on her arms and wept. She was still flat on the edge of the cliff, with Amir balancing on the ledge.

In a minute she calmed down and reassured Amir. "I'm sorry, I'm sorry. I'm going to get you up now."

She looked around her. Lokka's tree stared forlornly back at her, the remains of his meal still stuck in the branches. She dragged her eyes away and thought hard. She was going to need a rope to pull Amir up but there was nothing she could fashion into one up here. She went back to the edge and crouched down.

"I'm going to run down to my village and get a rope," she said. "I'll be very, very quick, okay?"

"NO!" Amir's scream bounced off the cliff. "No, please don't go. Don't leave me."

"I can't get you up without one, Amir. I'll be back before you know it. You'll be fine."

Selvi ran off before he could say anything else, though it broke her heart to see how terrified he was. They always had a spare coil of rope at the back by the well, so she raced all the way home to get it.

Her mother looked up, startled, as she ran past without a word, breathless from the long run. Selvi picked up the rope and rushed off again, leaving her mother open-mouthed with confusion.

Amir was still there when she got back, clinging on for dear life.

"I'm here," she said, dragging the rope to the plateau. She tied one end to Lokka's tree and dropped the other end over the edge, moving it until it was right next to Amir. "Here, grab hold of this."

Amir grasped the rope and swung against the rock, hitting his cheek.

"Put your feet flat on the rock, then start moving." She coaxed him up with her words. "One hand over the other, up and up. Use your feet to walk up the rock."

Somehow—slowly, painfully—Amir made it back up to the plateau. He kneeled down and put his head on the ground in relief. Selvi felt like crying herself. They'd done it! They'd fallen off the cliff at the edge of the world and lived to tell the tale.

If only Lokka were here too . . . She felt the tears come again and wiped them away quickly.

"I'm sorry," said Amir.

"It's not your fault." She gulped and looked away from him.

"It is. I was the one who took us over the cliff in the first place. And all the other stuff with Ravindu. And now Lokka's disappeared."

"I just don't understand." Selvi couldn't stop the sob escaping, and her tears spilled freely again. "You can't just *lose* a leopard."

"Selvi, um . . ." Amir cleared his throat a few times, as if working up the courage to say something. "I think . . . um, even though we didn't see it, I think it's most likely that—"

"No!" She didn't want to hear it. She got up and looked out over the mountain ridge. A family of gray langurs swung across the trees on a slope on the other side. She turned back to Amir. "I've lost him. But I'm not going to rest until I find him again."

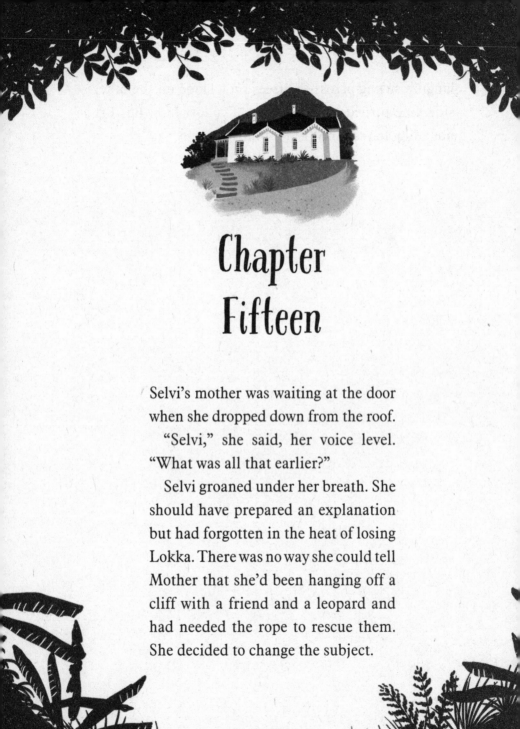

Chapter Fifteen

Selvi's mother was waiting at the door when she dropped down from the roof.

"Selvi," she said, her voice level. "What was all that earlier?"

Selvi groaned under her breath. She should have prepared an explanation but had forgotten in the heat of losing Lokka. There was no way she could tell Mother that she'd been hanging off a cliff with a friend and a leopard and had needed the rope to rescue them. She decided to change the subject.

"Are you going out, Mother?"

Her mother shook her head impatiently. "*We* are going out. Have you forgotten about Uncle's? I've been waiting for you and then you run off with a rope and now you look filthy. Go quickly, have a wash and change so we can leave. Uncle is going to be angry that we're late, but you can't turn up looking like that."

Selvi rushed inside, grateful that there was no time for more questions. Hopefully Mother would be in too much of a hurry to ask her again. She ached for Lokka as she splashed water rock.

They hurried down the path to Uncle's, walking very fast. Selvi kept looking out over the slopes, hoping for a glimpse of the beloved spotted coat.

Uncle lived in a big house on the top of a hill overlooking a vast area of green mountainside. There were steps cut into the hill as well as a long curving drive for his carriage. No wonder the villagers referred to him as the king of the mountains.

The wide, tiled roof and whitewashed walls of the house looked beautiful against the surrounding green hills. Selvi and her mother went in through the open front door, Mother already shrinking at the thought of his disapproval.

Selvi turned and looked out through the front door.

She wished she was outside, at the plateau, searching for Lokka. But she shuffled in with her mother, her mind full of thoughts about the leopard's inexplicable disappearance.

Mother nudged her and she realized that Uncle had spoken to her. He was sitting in a large recliner chair, his eyes hooded. She smiled. She never said much but she was nice.

Mother nudged Selvi again and looked at her expectantly.

"Er," she said. "I'm very well, thank you." She hoped that was what he'd asked her.

Uncle sighed, and Mother flushed with shame. "Since you turned up late," he said to Mother, "we'll eat at once." His wife went off to tell the housekeeper.

As Uncle talked, Selvi's thoughts drifted back to the cliff. It finally hit her what had happened, and she began shaking at the thought of the three of them clinging on to the cliff. It was nothing short of a miracle that they were alive. But Lokka was gone. If she knew that he'd fallen off the cliff that would have brought some closure. But her heart told her he hadn't and the mystery of his loss was agony.

Selvi found herself sitting at the large dining table with her mother, uncle, and aunty. The table was covered with oval dishes of the tiniest samba rice, deep bowls of flaming-orange sambals and bright mallungs, chunks of fish in milky gravy, and strips of crispy pappadums. Selvi suddenly realized how hungry she was. Sea fish was a luxury in her part of the island, being in the interior of Serendib and high up in the mountains, but it was an everyday food for her uncle.

Maybe if they ate fast they could go home sooner, and Selvi would have time to go looking for Lokka. She served herself quickly, dumping big spoonfuls of rice and curries on her plate. She ate ravenously, savoring the beautifully spiced curries that blended perfectly with the crunch of coconut and leafy greens in the rice. Half a plate left; she'd finish soon and they could leave.

She sensed the silence and looked up, halfway through a big mouthful. Mother was staring at her in horror, frozen in the act of helping herself to some food. Selvi looked at the others' plates. No one had even started eating. She munched down her mouthful and swallowed quickly, mortified. What had she done?

"Are you not feeding her?" said Uncle to Mother. There was a silence, and Selvi wasn't sure if she was supposed to say something. Her face burned with embarrassment.

"Never mind, let's just eat," said Aunty. She began a conversation about some drought in the north of the island to take the focus off what had happened.

The rest of the evening was strained after that. Mother was upset and confused, and Selvi felt ashamed for making her so. She let the conversation wash over her, smiling stiffly and nodding while she thought only about her missing leopard.

It felt as if they were there for hours. It was dark by the time they took their leave. "I agree, it's a good idea," Mother was saying to Uncle as they stood at the doorstep. She smiled down at Selvi. "Don't you think so?"

Selvi nodded, her mind spinning with different possibilities for where Lokka was as she looked out into the gathering darkness.

Uncle sent them home in his carriage. Mother spoke gently to Selvi as they were trundling down the mountain paths in the dark.

"What's going on?" she said, taking Selvi's hand. "You're not like yourself at all these days."

Selvi didn't know what to say. Should she confide in Mother? No, she'd be too concerned for Selvi and would stop her from leaving her sight. She hated worrying her mother like this. She didn't even look upset any more. Just concerned.

Selvi turned away and looked out at the ghostly shapes of trees on the slopes whizzing by. "It's nothing, Mother. Everything is fine."

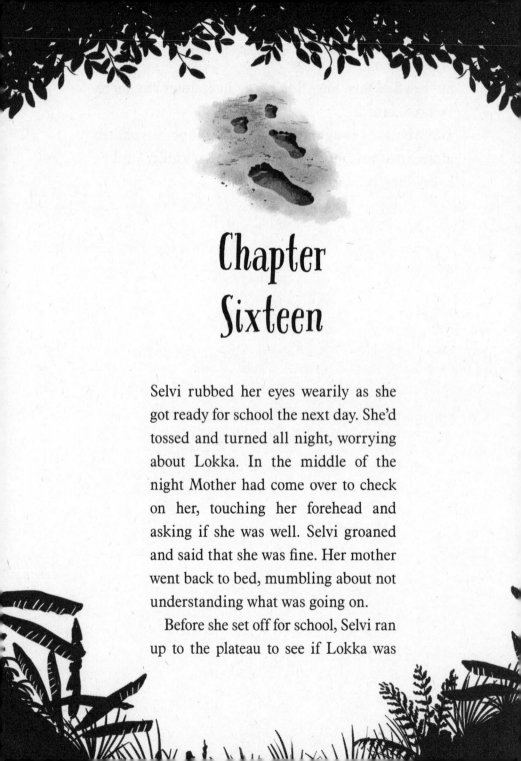

Chapter Sixteen

Selvi rubbed her eyes wearily as she got ready for school the next day. She'd tossed and turned all night, worrying about Lokka. In the middle of the night Mother had come over to check on her, touching her forehead and asking if she was well. Selvi groaned and said that she was fine. Her mother went back to bed, mumbling about not understanding what was going on.

Before she set off for school, Selvi ran up to the plateau to see if Lokka was there. It looked hauntingly lonely in the early morning light. Lokka's tree was empty and the carcass of the animal on the branches had fallen off and been carried away by jackals. There was an impression of Lokka on the sand from yesterday that made her breath catch in her throat. There were also big footprints all over the place.

Jansz.

Selvi ran up and down the mountains, looking for Lokka. The sambar looked up at the sound of her jingling anklets as she called his name. But they were used to her and continued grazing on the slope undisturbed.

Eventually Selvi ran out of time and had to trudge down to school. She sat miserably in the corner while the classroom filled up. Minoli glanced at her as she sat down in her row. "Are you all right?"

At first Selvi didn't realize she was talking to her. She tried to smile at Minoli. "I've just lost something special, that's all," she said.

"I hope you find it soon then," said Minoli, prodding her lunch pack through a hole in her tattered bag. "Do you want me to help you look?"

"No, but thank you."

"Ugh," she said, distracted as she fiddled with her bag and giving Selvi an idea. "I've mended this so many times it's falling apart now."

Miss Heba started the lesson, and to Selvi's intense irritation there was a growl from Amir's side of the room. Thankfully the teacher seemed to share her annoyance, because she glared at the children.

"Come on, not this again," said Miss Heba. "This is getting old now, Amir, Ravindu."

"It wasn't me, miss," said Amir.

Miss Heba looked to the back where Amir was sitting. "Sorry, I'd forgotten you've changed places. Ravindu, please stop it."

"Miss, I was just wondering something," said Ravindu, looking sneakily at Selvi. "How many leopards do we have in Serendib?"

The class looked up with interest at this. Selvi put her head in her hands. She didn't know what Ravindu was playing at, but she didn't like whatever it was.

Miss Heba put her chalk down. Usually this was what Selvi loved about her teacher. She didn't like being disturbed but if there was a topic that everyone was interested in, she'd stop the lesson and discuss it. "I don't think we know exactly," she said. "But there are lots. We have them all over the island. Here in the mountains, the rainforests, the dry-zone forests. Pretty much everywhere."

"Has the number not gone down, then?" said Amir. "Because of those people who hunt them to sell?"

"Poachers? I'm sure they're having an impact. We just don't have the numbers to prove it."

"There was one that came to our village," said a girl at the back. "And the villagers killed it."

"That's different, Mayuri." Miss Heba looked at her kindly. "As the number of people increases and we spread out all over the land, the leopards' territories shrink. So sometimes they accidentally wander into villages and the people get scared."

"There's no need to get scared," said Salma, from the front row, stroking the kitten on her lap. "I saw one really close up once, but they don't mean us any harm."

Miss Heba smiled. "You're quite right, Salma."

"Do you think it's right that the Queen has outlawed killing leopards, miss?" said Ravindu. "Given that there are so many of them."

Selvi couldn't understand his stupid questioning. Of course it was right! The animals were just minding their own business, living their lives.

Miss Heba looked at him thoughtfully. "What do *you* think? You tell *me*."

"Killing is bad. But, I don't know . . . I mean, if hunting helps people who need it earn money. And Serendib has so many leopards . . ."

Selvi felt her blood boil but Miss Heba interrupted Ravindu just as he was trailing off. "I'd like you to think about that a bit more, actually. It's a good discussion to have. I don't know what this new obsession is, and we don't have time at the moment. But I think we should talk about it another time. School finishes for the holidays on Wednesday, so let's do it then."

"I'd like that," said Salma.

"Why do some leopards have gold rings round their spots, miss?" said Ravindu, with another glance at Selvi.

Selvi stared at him, hardly daring to breathe. What was he doing! How could he mention Lokka after everything?

"I don't think there's such a thing. Not that I've heard of," said Miss Heba.

"Yes, there is! I've heard of one. His coat is really special, with his spots outlined in gold. I mean fuzzy, soft gold." He turned to Selvi innocently. "I think Selvi might know him?"

She ignored him. Miss Heba made an *ooh* with her mouth. "I hope he stays away then, for his own good."

"Why, miss?" said Minoli.

"Well, if this leopard is as you say, that sounds highly unusual. Rare always means lots of money."

"How so, miss?" Amir asked from the back.

"People will pay most for something only a few people can have. If this leopard has a particularly beautiful coat that has never been seen before, it'll fetch a high price."

Selvi leaned back, her thoughts spinning like a mountain storm. So that was why the men were so keen to get Lokka! It was why, in spite of everything, they wanted him, and him only. Lokka was the most endangered leopard in Serendib.

And she'd lost him.

Chapter Seventeen

Once school had ended, Selvi stalked off home alone. Minoli had tried to talk to her, and not even about anything to do with Ravindu, which she was surprised about. But she was losing time and had to carry on looking for Lokka so she made an excuse and left.

But—of course—Amir caught up with her before she'd gone very far. This had become a daily ritual and it looked as if he wasn't giving up, even after all that'd happened. She slowed down briefly to give him a chance to catch up and then continued on her way.

"Hey, wait!" he hollered after her. "I'm coming to look for Lokka too."

Selvi sighed and stopped. Amir came blundering up, grasping foliage to pull himself along. They continued on, as Selvi kept a watchful eye out for any flash of her beloved spotted leopard.

"Selvi?" said Amir as she scanned the horizon for Lokka.

"What?" She moved toward the wilderness on the hills to the west. Maybe she should check there.

Amir was running to keep up with her. "I just wondered . . . We're okay, aren't we?"

Selvi stopped and turned to him. "What do you mean?"

"You're not mad at me, are you?"

Selvi laughed. There was something about him that made it difficult to stay angry with him for long.

"Let me tell you something, Amir." Selvi stopped near a large tree with pink blossoms snaking all over its thick trunk. "Do you remember when we were on the plateau and you admitted you'd told Ravindu everything and then he'd passed that information on to Jansz?"

"Y-es?" Amir grimaced.

"I thought to myself, well, that's okay because this is as bad as it gets, he couldn't make things *any worse* if he tried." She paused. "Do you know what happened next?"

Amir scratched his head. "What?"

"You threw us over a cliff. We were hanging by our hands above a vertical drop."

Amir covered his face and groaned. "I do ruin everything, don't I?"

Selvi laughed. "Yes, you do. But you know what, I don't think you can have a near-death experience with someone, escape together, and not be friends with them anymore."

"Phew. Thank you. I guess that means we're okay?" he said hopefully.

"We are. Sure, you're a bit incompetent. Bumbling. Can't keep your mouth shut."

"Okay, okay, I get it." Amir shoved her hard but playfully and ran off. "Race you to the other side."

Selvi yelled and bolted after him, screaming with laughter as they sprinted down the hill to the forest. They combed through the trees together, looking for Lokka. Both Selvi and Amir knew how elusive leopards were, but they even managed to spot two others in the distance. There was no sign of Lokka anywhere.

"I'm sure he'd show himself if he was around," said Selvi as they walked around in the increasing darkness under the canopy of trees. Even though she'd started out feeling positive, she felt glummer as the afternoon wore on and they didn't spot him anywhere.

"I don't know," said Amir, stopping and peering into a hollow trunk. "I feel like we're wasting time looking here. We need to figure out what actually *happened* to him."

Selvi had to agree. There was a limit to how far and wide they could look for him. The truth was, they were searching blindly and she wasn't sure this was the way to go about it. "You're right. Let's get out of here."

They trudged back up the hill to their part of the mountains as the surroundings gradually darkened around them. In the distance, they caught a glimpse of Jansz and Liyanage walking together, probably searching for the same thing as them.

"Let's talk tomorrow and come up with a plan," she said to Amir as they stopped near the track going up to his house. "I should get back before Mother worries." She walked back home slowly, her thoughts heavy and jumbled.

As she got home, Mother was standing on the doorstep, looking out into the night. "Selvi! Where have you been?"

Selvi gulped as she looked at her mother's drawn face. She hadn't realized how late it was. "I was just . . . just walking around." She couldn't bear her mother's disappointment so she went quickly inside. The house smelled of freshly boiled kadala.

"This won't do at all," said Mother, following her inside. "I'm so worried about you!"

"Please, Mother. I'm fine. I just lost track of time." To avoid having to answer questions she got ready to sleep quickly and curled up on her mat even while her belly rumbled for the kadala.

The next morning Mother was sitting on the mat with her sewing. Rectangles of colored cotton were strewn around her and she was sewing two of them together. "Would you have any leftover bits of cloth that you don't need, Mother?" asked Selvi, remembering Minoli's school bag.

"I have loads in there," she said, nodding toward an overstuffed bag spilling over with bits of fabric. "I always collect them but I don't know how useful such small pieces would be." Selvi pulled out an armful and sat next to her mother, sorting them into similar colors and patterns. She found one that had quite a few pieces she could sew together and, borrowing one of Mother's needles and some thread, began to stitch.

"What are you making?" said Mother, stacking up a pile of neatly hemmed pieces.

"A school bag. I think I'll be able to make quite a big piece of material by joining these blue bits together."

"But your bag is still brand new."

"It's not for me, it's for a girl who sits next to me in school." Selvi slipped the threaded needle into the fabric and pulled it out the other side. "Her bag's full of holes so I think she might like a new one."

Mother smiled. "That's nice of you. I'm sure she'll be very happy."

"Hopefully it won't take too long. I'll do a bit every day so that I can give it to her on the last day of term."

"I've got to go out now," said Mother, getting up and neatening the place. "There's breakfast in the kitchen. Make sure you eat before you go out."

For the next three days Selvi and Amir searched around Lokka's plateau area.

Selvi didn't dare climb back down the cliff, but they hunted for clues for what might have happened to him.

They examined the ground, looked for tracks, climbed the trees and scoured the surroundings.

They found nothing.

"Where is he?" Selvi dropped to the ground in frustration. She opened the food parcel she'd brought with her, and Amir came over to share it. They sat and ate their squares of coconut sweets in silence, gazing out over the horizon and the many levels of the green mountain range.

She ducked when she spotted movement on the other side. "Quick!" she said to Amir, gesturing to him and crawling over to the base of Lokka's tree where they wouldn't be seen. "Ravindu's by the waterfall."

They spied on him while covered by the tree. Ravindu was on his own, skulking around at the bottom of the waterfall and eventually walking through the stream until he was out of sight.

Selvi turned and leaned against the tree. She tossed the last sweet to Amir and swept up the crumbs from the bag into her mouth. "Everyone's looking for him," she said gloomily as she munched. "But no one's any closer."

"I've just realized something," said Amir. "It's only two more days to Thursday."

"Jansz's cut-off date. I know."

"I saw him first thing this morning, searching near the caves."

"I can imagine." Selvi rubbed her forehead. "I've seen him and his goons several times in the last few days. I don't think they'll give up, even if they don't find him by Thursday."

"I think they'll give one last big push though."

Selvi sat up at that. Amir's words had given her an idea.

"What is it?" he said.

Selvi got up and dusted her skirt. "I realized something when we were talking to Miss Heba the other day. Lokka will always be sought after. Jansz won't ever stop looking for him. Even if they don't find him in time for the buyer they've got, they won't leave him alone. There'll always be another buyer for him."

Amir slouched down. "It's useless, isn't it?"

"Not necessarily. What I mean is, we might all be looking for Lokka for different reasons, but the end result is we're all looking for him."

"So one of us will eventually find him if he's alive?"

"Exactly. And because it's a question of money and time, I think Jansz will probably find him first."

"So what do we do?"

"We follow them. We shadow them day and night, and they'll lead us straight to Lokka."

Chapter Eighteen

Minoli slid into Selvi's row, squeezing past another girl until she was sitting beside her. "Last day of term!" she said, clutching the bottom of her bag so that things didn't fall out. "How are you?"

"Could be better." Selvi pulled out the bag that she'd completed last night. "Here."

Minoli took it and unrolled it on her lap, frowning. She looked up at Selvi.

"My mother does lots of sewing and has loads of scrap material. I thought I'd make some into a bag for you."

Minoli looked at the bag again, not saying anything. She ran her fingers over the soft new fabric and traced the bright pattern. At last she said, "You're very kind, Selvi."

"It's nothing," said Selvi, a bit embarrassed. She was glad to see the teacher come in at that moment.

Miss Heba announced that it was the day of the leopard discussion. Selvi had forgotten about that, and it looked as if Ravindu had too, because he squeaked and looked up in alarm.

"I hope you're ready, Ravindu," said Miss Heba. She came around her desk and sat at the edge. "You can go first. Tell us why you think killing leopards is a good idea."

The class laughed.

Ravindu blushed as he stood up. "It sounds bad when you put it like that!"

"It's what it is," muttered Minoli.

Miss Heba heard her and nodded. "I agree, actually."

"I just think," said Ravindu, shrugging, "that *people* are more important."

"In what way, though?" *said* Amir, glaring at him from the back row. "If there were no other living things left on Earth but us, we wouldn't survive either. We need the others."

"But I'm talking about *one* species. I'm not saying we should wipe them all out. I just think it's fine to reduce their numbers. They're pests."

"Come on!" said a boy sitting near Ravindu. "It's not their fault. My grandfather said that when he was a boy nobody lived in these parts. Now we have little villages all over their territory."

"It must be confusing for the wildlife," said Amir. "Once they could go wherever they wanted and then suddenly they're pests."

"Good point," said Miss Heba, nodding at Amir. Ravindu glared at this sign of approval from Miss Heba.

His friend Priyanka jumped in. "We can't help some things. Humans are here now and we can't just go away. We have to manage the threat from leopards."

"Very few leopards are actually killed for being a danger to villagers," said Minoli. "Most of them stay away, as you well know. Think about it, we live in a place full of leopards, but how often do we see them?"

"Exactly!" said Amir. "So they manage themselves. We don't have to manage them."

"People need money to *live*," said Priyanka. "I can't see why a few leopards getting killed is a bad thing, if they can earn a bit of money by it."

"That's what I think too," said Ravindu. "I'm not saying to wipe them all out!"

"Where does it end though?" said one of the little

ones in the front. "If you say killing them is okay, then they will all die in the end."

"Not really," said Ravindu, though he looked a bit less sure of himself. "That's not going to happen so easily."

"They're just like my cat," said Salma, holding up her kitten for Ravindu to see. "Just bigger."

Ravindu stared at the kitten for a few moments as it peered around the room, and looked away.

"I just think," he said, his voice sounding much quieter, "we needn't worry about numbers. We have loads of them."

"That's the stupidest thing I've ever heard!" blurted out Selvi. She went red as she realized that everyone was staring at her. She hadn't meant to erupt like that, or even join in at all, but now that she'd started she couldn't stop. "Yes, there are loads *now*. But someday there'll be lots more of us, and far fewer of them. Can you imagine what the future will be like if we carry on hunting?"

Ravindu looked thoughtful. Priyanka shrugged.

Selvi hadn't finished yet. "Jungles will become smaller. And animals like Lok—animals like leopards will be nearly gone and only live in special places and people would have to come from far and wide to see them because they're so rare. They'll live in cages or specially protected forests." She blinked back tears. "Can you *imagine* a world like that?"

Miss Heba was looking at her intently. "You're quite right, Selvi." She paused for a bit and then said, "Do you think people don't understand how important this is for you?"

Selvi nodded and brushed her eyes with the back of her hand.

"I don't like that picture," said Salma. "That sounds horrible. I like how it is now."

Miss Heba nodded at her.

"I don't like it either," said Minoli.

Several heads around the class were nodding. The children had gone quiet, and a couple of them had their chins in their hands.

"We just need to change our thinking," said Amir. "I know I have. I think we should be more like Selvi."

Selvi looked at him in surprise, and blushed. "Yes!" said Minoli. "I'm with that. Be more like Selvi."

"That's a nice note to end on," said Miss Heba, getting up and going behind her desk. "We should get to our arithmetic now, then that's it for the next two weeks!"

The class settled down and Selvi pulled out her books. She felt that that had gone well. She couldn't, however, help but notice the look of utter dejection on Ravindu's face. He caught her eye and, for some reason she couldn't understand, mouthed the word *sorry* and looked away.

Chapter Nineteen

"Jansz is going to love this plan," said Amir as they came to the track leading down to the village. He plucked at a tree fern and fiddled with it, chomping it in his mouth as they set off down the path. "He's already really fed up with you."

Selvi shrugged and carried on walking. The ground was still slippery with mud after the torrential rains last night. Patches of moss draped the gray, woody branches on her side, and cuplike leaf formations reached for the sky. "I'm hoping he won't know what we're up to!" She stopped at a rock pool Lokka sometimes drank at. The sight of it filled her with sadness. She'd always found it amusing to see such a large cat dip his tongue so delicately into water to drink, but, unlike humans, leopards weren't able to suck up water with their mouths.

"There's another . . ." She trailed off as she spotted something.

It was Jansz, walking on the opposite side of the stream with Liyanage. They went up the path talking, Liyanage gesturing with his hands.

"This makes me really nervous," said Amir. "If they catch us—"

Selvi shushed him and darted after the men. After a beat, Amir followed.

"Listen," he said. "If we get caught, you just run. I'm not in any trouble with them so I'll be able to talk my way out of it."

Selvi looked at him gratefully. "Thank you," she said, "but hopefully that won't be necessary. We don't have to go close—unless they find Lokka, of course."

The men were still talking in low voices as they walked along. Selvi knew this path well. It led to the bottom of the waterfall. The children followed at a distance, careful to keep themselves hidden behind trees.

Jansz and Liyanage spent some time inspecting the ground near the waterfall, then looking all around and up at the trees purposefully.

"What are they doing?" whispered Selvi. "I wish we could hear what they're saying."

The sound of the gushing water drowned out any chance of that.

"Be careful," said Amir, holding her arm as she strained closer. "You don't want them to see us."

"But I need to know what they're doing." Selvi shrugged herself free as an idea occurred to her. "I have to hear what they're saying."

"Don't, Selvi! You'd have to be standing next to them to hear anything."

"I know," she said, darting off. "So that's exactly what I'm going to do."

Chapter Twenty

Selvi crept away from the men, skirting them in a wide circle as she ducked behind foliage so they wouldn't see her. The greenery rustled wildly in her wake as if a buffalo was powering through behind her. She turned back and glared at Amir, who raised a hand in apology. Luckily the roar of the water covered any sounds, and the men didn't see him.

Jansz and Liyanage were sitting on rocks near the waterfall, looking defeated. The air here was damp and misty. Once the water reached the ground, it flowed on in a shallow stream, turning a corner and disappearing from view. Selvi crossed where the men couldn't see her, deftly jumping from one wet brown stone to the next as the water swirled around them.

She crept around the far bank, Amir still following. Selvi kept hidden behind trees and eyed the men through the gaps between them as she rustled along. She went right up to the other side of the waterfall.

"What are you doing now?" Amir hissed.

Selvi pointed behind the curtain of water. There was a narrow space between it and the rock wall it was gushing down.

Amir's eyes went wide, but before he could say anything Selvi slipped into the gap. With a muttered oath, Amir followed her lead and stepped behind the curtain of water too.

The drumming of the water was furiously loud but the space was cool and echoey and the children inched closer to where the men were sitting.

". . . he was so sure he heard something . . ." The men's words came floating to them from beyond the noisy curtain. ". . . finally . . . maybe caught somewhere . . ."

Selvi finally came to a stop right next to the men.

They were barely four feet from them, separated only by a screen of water. Amir stopped next to her, breathing heavily.

"We can't let anyone know about this leopard," came Jansz's voice through the hiss of water. "I don't want any competition."

Liyanage sucked his teeth. "The boss is going to come down hard on us if we don't get it in time."

"So we have to try even harder. It's annoying that he wants it alive. So much easier to shoot it than trap it. But there's more money if he sells it as an exotic pet instead of a skin."

"Well, it's clearly not here," sighed Liyanage. "I think the boy was mistaken."

Selvi wiped spray off her face. *The boy?* She remembered Ravindu scouting the area and she wondered if this was something to do with him. Had he seen Lokka? She glanced quizzically at Amir, but he looked deathly anxious.

Come on, he mouthed. *Let's go.*

The spray was drenching them and the sound of the water was drumming into Selvi's brain. She tried to shake off Amir, who kept patting her to make her leave. Through the sound of the water and Amir's fidgeting she heard something else. Something small and thin and so low she couldn't be sure she hadn't imagined it. Amir gestured back the way they'd come with his thumb and tried to pull her away. She waved him off and closed her eyes, listening hard. She tuned out the sound of Jansz's muttering and focused her mind.

There it was again. What on earth? Selvi looked all around her but there was nothing but rock behind her, stretching high into the sky. There'd been a rockfall to one side, but other than that it was all quite undisturbed. The space they were in was tall but snug, with only a small gap between the rock and water. There didn't seem to be anywhere for something to hide.

Amir was getting increasingly jittery. He kept tapping her arm and gesturing for them to leave. She threw her hands up in annoyance. "Stop it!" she snapped at him. "We're here for a reason!"

"You're going to get us caught!" said Amir. He turned to go in a huff and promptly slipped on the rock, falling through the curtain of water and disappearing from Selvi's view.

Chapter Twenty-One

There was an unceremonious splash as Amir fell through the waterfall into the stream beyond. Selvi smacked her head with her hand in exasperation and slipped back the way she'd come. She fled into the trees and up the path, climbing steadily away, remembering Amir's words about letting the men find only him if they got caught.

When she was high enough to feel sure they couldn't catch her, she watched what was happening below.

She couldn't hear what they were all saying, but it seemed quite cheerful and Liyanage even looked as if he was laughing. Only Jansz was silent, studying Amir, who was chatting and waving his arms about.

She decided to wait for him, absolutely bursting to tell him what she'd heard. After a few minutes he turned up, soaking wet.

"What did you tell them you were doing?" she asked, unable to help herself laughing at him.

He grinned. "I said I'd forgotten a shoe last time I came swimming and I was looking for it when I fell in."

"Did they buy it?"

"I think so," he said as they walked on, his shirt stuck to his back. "Liyanage did, at least."

"I noticed Jansz didn't say much."

Amir bit his lip. "I think he recognized me from when he saw me at my house. But that doesn't mean anything, does it?"

"No," said Selvi. "It doesn't." All the same, she was a bit uneasy. She didn't want Jansz connecting the two of them. The last thing she wanted was for Amir to be in trouble too.

"Anyway, I have big news," she said. "Did you hear that noise when we were behind the waterfall?"

Amir shivered in his wet clothes. "No? And why do you look so happy?"

They'd come to the track that led to his house. Selvi laughed, her heart soaring.

"Because I know where Lokka is!"

Chapter
Twenty-Two

"Tell me then!" said Amir, all agog. "Quick! I'm shivering and need to get home to change."

"When we were at the waterfall," said Selvi, "I heard the sound of a very soft growl over the water. I think it was Lokka. Actually, I *know* it was Lokka. I'd recognize his voice anywhere."

"What?" Amir held out his palms confusedly, as if asking for more. "But where? Jansz would have found him if he was there."

"There'd been a rockfall behind the waterfall. I think he's trapped there."

Amir shook his head. "But how could he get there? Have you forgotten that we last saw him hanging halfway down a cliff?"

Selvi laughed again. She felt so much lighter now that she knew Lokka wasn't dead. "My guess is that there was a fissure or something in the ledge that we didn't notice, and he managed to crawl into it. Maybe it led to a cave or passage of some sort in the rock. What if the exit's blocked by that rockfall and now he's stuck? He could have been looking for a way out all this time. He's got to be behind those rocks."

"Do you think he's okay?"

Selvi had been wondering the same thing. "He's probably not hungry, as he'd just eaten a large meal when he fell off the ledge, remember? I think he can go days without food or water. I just hope he's not hurt in any way. And he must be very frightened." Selvi's heart clenched at the thought.

"We saw Ravindu at the waterfall yesterday!" said Amir. "He must have heard something and told Jansz."

She nodded. "I think it was harder for Lokka to be heard today because of the heavy rain last night. The waterfall is raging now. We only heard him because we were *behind* the water."

"The rat!" said Amir.

Selvi sighed. "Ravindu must have told Jansz that Lokka was near the waterfall and then regretted it, because he said sorry to me today at school but I didn't know what for. Now I do."

"Should we go back now to get Lokka out?"

Selvi looked up at the darkening sky. All she wanted to do was rush back and try to dig Lokka out with her bare hands. But they had to be careful. "We can't do anything with Jansz there. If he sees me he'll know something's up at once. And it sounds as if he's becoming suspicious of you too."

Selvi didn't want to leave Lokka there for a moment longer, but she didn't have any choice. And once she went home, her mother would never let her leave the house in the dark. She'd have to come back early in the morning and free him.

"I think Lokka will be fine for the night," she said to Amir. "There's no school tomorrow so meet me near the waterfall first thing and we'll get him out then."

Amir gave her a thumbs-up and ran down the track to his house. Selvi started off home with a new determination.

Tomorrow she was going to find her lost leopard!

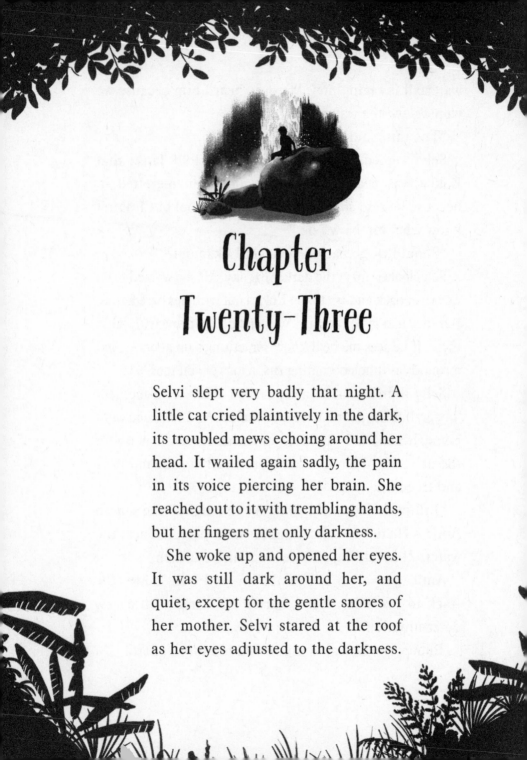

Chapter Twenty-Three

Selvi slept very badly that night. A little cat cried plaintively in the dark, its troubled mews echoing around her head. It wailed again sadly, the pain in its voice piercing her brain. She reached out to it with trembling hands, but her fingers met only darkness.

She woke up and opened her eyes. It was still dark around her, and quiet, except for the gentle snores of her mother. Selvi stared at the roof as her eyes adjusted to the darkness.

She was safe at home with her family. Would Lokka be okay? She'd been so happy that they'd found him and knew he was alive that she hadn't thought much beyond that. But would he be frightened and confused, trapped in the darkness? She knew she was being silly—he was a night animal after all, always prowling about in the dark. But what if he'd known she was there yesterday, so close to him and yet doing nothing to release him? Maybe the leopard had heard her voice and now he was waiting and waiting, confused and hurt that she hadn't come to rescue him when she knew he was trapped there.

She rolled over and saw the dark shape of her mother on her mat on the other side of the room. It was all peaceful and still, but her mind was at the waterfall, churning with the din of the falling water.

As soon as she saw the tiniest sign of dawn, Selvi was up and rolling her mat away.

She crept out and ran toward the waterfall, hoping Amir would be there soon. The path looked a bit scary when it was barely light. She'd never been out this early in the morning before. The chill crept inside her, but she crossed her arms tight and ran on. A chattering came from a beraliya tree on her right and its branches shuffled as she went past. She didn't wait to see what was there and moved rapidly on, only stopping when she came to the waterfall.

The last of the moonlight shone on the water, highlighting the stones speckling its path. Behind it the waterfall roared, the sound seeming even clearer and more peaceful than before.

Amir was sitting on the rock that Jansz had been on the night before, waiting for her. He looked up when she approached. "You couldn't sleep either?"

Selvi shook her head, suddenly overcome. The sight of him sitting there, waiting patiently for her, moved her in a way she couldn't explain. She thought she was alone in her love for Lokka. But it looked as if Amir had come to feel the same way too.

He stood up as Selvi stepped past and they both slipped behind the curtain of water.

"Lokka?" called Selvi. "It's me. Are you there?"

There was a scraping, scrabbling sound, and a growl came from behind the rockfall.

"Lokka! It *is* you!" Selvi was overjoyed. "Don't worry, we're here and we've come to get you out."

She stood back and looked at the rocks in the semi-darkness. Massive boulders stood in front of her, seemingly fixed to the ground. She levered her feet against the side of one and pushed with all her might. She didn't feel even the slightest give. Amir did the same, and then they pushed together.

"I don't think these have been moved in a long time," said Amir. Sweat glistened on his face in the half-light.

Selvi sighed and rubbed her forehead. Who was she fooling? For all she knew, the stones had been here for hundreds of years and were all but welded to the earth now. Even with Amir's help there was no way they could move them.

What on earth were they going to do?

Chapter Twenty-Four

Lokka gave another roar from behind the stones.

Selvi could picture him on the other side, standing alert with his tail curling in the air.

"We're coming, Lokka. Just trying to work out how to get to you." She bent down and gripped a rock hard, spreading her arms wide to hug it. She pulled, straining to make it move.

The two children tugged at the rocks. They pushed them. They kicked them in frustration, hurting their toes. Nothing made a difference.

Selvi was sweating now too, in spite of the coldness of the early morning.

Think, Selvi, think!

They didn't have the strength to do it this way, so she had to think of something different. She stood there looking at the stones, panicking now as she realized how impossible their task was. What if Jansz came back this very minute? They had to be quick but they didn't have a clue.

Lokka roared as if encouraging her on.

"I'm thinking, I'm thinking!" she called out. "Give me a minute."

So if strength wasn't the answer, what was? The one skill she had was climbing, but that wasn't going to help her here.

Or was it?

Selvi stepped back and squinted at the pile of rocks. There were smaller stones at the top. What if she were to dislodge one of those? Could she make a space? A space big enough for a leopard to leap through?

Amir followed her gaze and his face lit up.

Excited now, Selvi began to climb. The rocks were completely smooth, and it took her a while to get the hang of climbing them. She had to create a kind of suction with her hands and feet, like rock frogs did. Soon she was at the top, perched on a few of the smaller stones.

Amir was looking up at her, his face hopeful.

She found a stone that was a bit smaller than the others and pushed it sideways. It gave very slightly, and Selvi's heart lifted. "This looks promising," she called down, and then, "Nearly there, Lokka."

She pushed again. She didn't have to lift it or move it somewhere specific, just knock it down, and this made the task so much easier. "Get away, Amir!" she yelled, just as the stone shifted with a grinding sound. Amir jumped away, throwing himself through the waterfall and splashing out the other side. The stone crashed on to the ground below with a booming thud that echoed all around. A small space opened up in the rockfall, bringing with it the sharp cold and mossy dampness of the interior.

Before she knew it, there was a growl and Lokka leaped up, pushing his face through the gap. His body followed, pillowing out as he turned this way and that to get himself free. He stopped next to Selvi for a second as if to say thanks, and then in one fluid motion sprang down to the ground below. His claws clacked on the rock before he vaulted off again, slicing through the curtain of water. She heard Amir yelling in delight from the other side.

Selvi jumped down and threw herself through the cold waterfall, not caring about getting drenched. She was ecstatic. Lokka was free!

"Amir!" she cried. "Did you see—" She crashed to a halt at the scene that met her eyes.

Liyanage was standing ankle-deep in the stream, pointing his bow and arrow straight at Lokka, who was crouching in the stream where he'd landed, growling. The man let fly with an arrow and it whistled through the air straight toward the defenseless leopard.

Chapter Twenty-Five

Selvi screamed and threw herself toward Lokka. At the same time, the cat sprang sideways, knocking into Amir. The arrow whizzed harmlessly between them all.

Lokka leaped through the stream and away into the trees. Liyanage yelled in desperation and, turning to Selvi, shot a second arrow in her direction.

Selvi gasped and stumbled. The arrow had grazed the side of her shoulder, causing a sharp pain, and blood spilled down her sodden arm.

"WHAT ARE YOU DOING?" yelled Amir. He ran to Selvi.

"Oh, I have a plan, don't worry," Liyanage said. "Now we wait." He looked expectantly at the trees and, sure enough, Lokka appeared. He roared in anger and launched himself at Liyanage.

It might have been Liyanage's intention to lure Lokka back to help his friend, but in the face of an angry leopard, his plan seemed to fall apart. His hand shook with fear as he took aim again, and the arrow dropped harmlessly into the water.

Lokka swung at him, slashing his claws down Liyanage's cheek. Liyanage fell backward into the shallow water with a splash. Lokka stood over him and roared.

"NO, Lokka!" screamed Selvi. "No, *please!*"

Lokka turned to look at her, confused. Liyanage was a threat and needed to be stopped, but Selvi didn't seem happy with his actions. Well, if that's what she wanted, he'd back off, but he didn't have to like it. He slowly walked away from the man on the ground, growling gently.

Selvi nodded at him to reassure him. It was all right. She didn't want Liyanage to get hurt. She went up and stood next to Lokka, while Amir flanked him on the other side. "Leave this leopard alone!" said Selvi. "Or we won't be so merciful next time."

"Yes, Liyanage, get out before he kills you," said Amir.

Lokka snarled at the man, a long, low sound like a saw moving slowly through wood, as if adding his own warning.

Liyanage stood up slowly. He was wet and muddy, his cheek bleeding from Lokka's swipe. In spite of everything, there was a sneaky look in his eyes, as if he felt victory could still be his.

Before anyone knew what was happening, he snatched up his weapon and shot again at Lokka. This time the arrow nicked Lokka's ear and, roaring in pain, the leopard reared up.

Selvi and Amir both screamed but Lokka had had enough. He pounced on Liyanage, knocking him to the ground, and went straight for his throat.

Chapter Twenty-Six

"No, Lokka!" Selvi screamed. "NO!"
Amir had his hands over his eyes.

Selvi bent down and put a hand
on the leopard's back. It was the first
time she'd ever touched him. His fur
was thick and soft. She stroked him,
hoping to calm his anger and fear.

"Let's go," she said to Lokka sooth-
ingly. Lokka gently shook Selvi's hand
off his body, as if he'd made up his mind
what he needed to do. He growled and
went again for Liyanage's neck.

Selvi exclaimed and drew back in horror. Amir clutched her.

To Selvi's relief, Liyanage seemed unhurt, and it was his collar that Lokka was gripping. In one quick movement, the leopard dragged him out of the stream and over to a tall tree nearby. Lokka climbed up and up deftly, still dragging the hapless Liyanage with him, thumping him all over the tree. Lokka let go when he reached the highest branch, and Liyanage grabbed on to it for dear life.

With one last growl, Lokka climbed back down to the children, leaving the man clinging to the top of the tree.

"Wha—" Amir stared in astonishment.

Selvi began to laugh. She looked at Liyanage hanging on to his branch, alive but humiliated, and laughed even louder. Amir joined in when he realized what was going on. Lokka had used his food-protecting skills to put Liyanage somewhere he couldn't come back to pester them in a hurry.

Selvi bent down to look at Lokka's ear. She hoped he'd heal soon. She'd seen small injuries like this on him from time to time. She knew that leopards had to be on top form to be able to hunt successfully, and any injury that threatened that proficiency would cause them to waste away and die. It looked like he would always be missing a small piece of his ear, but she didn't think that would do him any harm.

She put both hands on the beautiful animal and closed her eyes, so thankful that he was safe and well after everything that had happened to him. She felt a rumbling coming from Lokka. If she didn't know that it was impossible for leopards to purr, she would have thought that was exactly what he was doing.

She opened her eyes and looked at where the arrow had grazed her arm. The blood had dried up and she felt fine. It was well into morning now and sunlight bounced off the stream and warmed the waterfall behind them. It was a new day, she and Amir had found Lokka and everything was all right now.

Amir was still laughing at Liyanage up in the tree. Langurs had come over and were looking curiously at him. "Look, he hasn't moved! Maybe he'll learn a lesson while he's up there waiting for someone to rescue him."

Selvi laughed. "Come on, let's get out of here. I think we should take Lokka to the plains on the south side of the mountain and leave him there for a while until we think of what to do."

"Good plan. Let's hurry before Jansz turns up." They turned to go, and Selvi gasped. They were too late. Jansz was heading straight toward them, a satisfied look on his face. Hurrying along beside him was Ravindu.

Chapter Twenty-Seven

"Well, well, well. What do we have here?" said Jansz as he splashed into the stream. He half grimaced, half smiled at them. "Thank you for finding my favorite leopard in the whole world."

Amir and Selvi stared with contempt at Ravindu, who'd stopped at the edge of the water and was looking on nervously.

"You're not getting him!" said Selvi. She looked to the leopard next to her. "Run, Lokka!"

Lokka growled at Jansz but stayed put. Selvi patted him gently. "Go!" she said. But she knew it was hopeless. After what had happened with Liyanage, Lokka wanted to stay and protect them.

Jansz laughed. "Well, what do you know? Everything I heard about that leopard is true."

"Your friend's over there," said Selvi, nodding toward the tree. "If you look carefully you'll see him on the highest branch."

Jansz snorted. "Fool belongs up there then. Looks like I have to do everything myself."

"You should just get lost unless you want to end up like Liyanage," said Amir. "Or worse."

"Shut up, boy," said Jansz, hardly looking at him. "I should have known you'd be with her. Hope she turns out to be a better friend than this one." He gestured toward Ravindu, who didn't look as if he was enjoying himself very much.

Selvi realized that Jansz was unarmed. Why was he standing there fearlessly? What was his game? Selvi couldn't figure it out. "What's going on?" she whispered to Amir.

He shrugged and looked at Selvi with fear in his eyes. Only Lokka seemed unconcerned, remaining fierce and alert as he faced Jansz.

"He's beautiful, isn't he?" said Jansz, eyeing Lokka greedily. "You won't believe it, but I have great respect for leopards."

Selvi spluttered. She was too outraged to even find the words.

"Sure you have," said Amir, rolling his eyes.

"It's true. I'm not the same as idiots like him up there." He pointed to Liyanage, who they could hear actually whimpering. "I'm new to this, but the boss has been teaching me how much these animals can do for us. He actually keeps a claw from *every* animal that we kill and sell. Says it's a sign of respect."

"That's not respect," said Selvi. She couldn't detest Jansz or his boss any more if she tried. "That's taking advantage for your own gain. *Killing* for your own gain!"

"Still," said Jansz. "I've come to be quite fond of the creatures." He looked almost misty-eyed. He came closer.

Selvi held her breath. Lokka stiffened. From the corner of her eye, she saw Ravindu shuffle his feet.

Still Jansz came nearer. He was smiling. He didn't stop until he was right in front of them, and then he suddenly grabbed Selvi with a meaty hand.

"You're coming with me, girl. I have something to show you." Selvi struggled and yelled as he pulled her away.

"Hey, let her go!" said Amir. "Unless you want the leopard on you."

"Oh, I'm not scared of the leopard," said Jansz, looking casually over his shoulder. "He can come too if he wants. Here, puss, come with us."

He continued to haul Selvi toward some trees on the other side of the path, taking a curving route around a little clearing.

Selvi began to get a very bad feeling. Jansz was up to something, but what was it? Why was he taunting Lokka like this? She tried to pull her arm away but his grip tightened. "It's right here," he said. "Just a few more steps."

She looked back at Lokka helplessly, trying to will the leopard to run away. But he was growling louder now, angry with the man for hurting his beloved friend. Suddenly he bounded toward Selvi, as if he couldn't stand by and do nothing any longer.

Jansz watched him approach. He smiled, a slow, satisfied smile that changed his face, and in that moment Selvi knew what he was up to.

"Noooooooooooo!" Selvi's scream echoed around the waterfall.

But it was too late. As Lokka reached them at speed, Jansz suddenly shoved Selvi to one side and jumped out of the way. Lokka's fierce expression turned to one of alarm as something closed over him and he was jerked sharply up into the air.

Chapter Twenty-Eight

Selvi and Amir raced over to where
Lokka was swinging from the tree in
a net. The frightened animal roared
and fought inside it, twisting and
turning as it tightened around him,
holding him captive. His fearful roars
tore right into Selvi's heart.

Amir tried to jump up to the net but
it swung way above his head.

Jansz laughed. "See, that wasn't
too hard, was it? I always knew I'd
get him in the end. And thanks to our

good friend Ravindu, we knew just where to lay the trap."

Ravindu stood rooted to the spot, his frightened eyes turned on Lokka thrashing about in the net. The leopard's roars even drowned out the noise of the waterfall.

"You'll never get away with this," said Selvi. The sight of her brave, loyal, magnificent leopard hanging in the air fighting for his life filled her with grief. But with it came a quiet, determined fury. She wasn't going to give up now. She would *never* give up fighting for Lokka. "I won't let you. I promise."

"Ah, now, don't go making promises you can't keep." Jansz smiled. "Now we've caught him, we won't be letting him go. He's the most difficult leopard we've ever trapped." He gazed admiringly at Lokka snarling and grunting in the net.

"This isn't over," said Amir.

"Oh, but I think it is. Though maybe not for *her*," said Jansz, and he mimed zipping his lips.

Selvi stared at him.

"What are you trying to say?" said Amir angrily. Jansz pretended to consider for a moment.

"All right then. A small reminder from me, girl. Remember I told you to keep out of our way or there'd be consequences? Well, you didn't listen, did you? So there *will* be consequences. In fact, they're happening as we speak."

The hot sunlight had dried Selvi's clothes and beat down relentlessly on her scalp, but inside a chill was beginning to grow. What did he mean . . . ?

Jansz looked up at Lokka. "I don't think the leopard is the only thing in trouble at the moment. You might want to head home, Selvi. Maybe your mother needs you?"

Selvi screamed. She made to leave, then stopped and looked at the leopard. Their eyes met, and he was the cat in her dreams again, pleading for help.

But she had to go. She turned around in anguish and ran home to her mother.

Chapter Twenty-Nine

Selvi raced all the way to her house. *Please let Mother be all right,* she repeated over and over inside her head as she flew down paths and vaulted over startled wildlife.

She got to the roof and dropped down in front of the house. What terrible thing was she going to find when she got inside? But her mother was standing at the door with a packed case in her hand. She looked unusually furious.

"Mother!" said Selvi. "Are you all right?"

"I should be asking *you* that. Where have you been?"

"Er . . . me?" asked Selvi, blinking in surprise.

"What is all this nonsense, Selvi? I don't know what's gotten into you lately. I've been waiting ages and Uncle is here with his carriage to take you away."

"What! Take me where?"

"To his house! We discussed it all and you agreed." Selvi gaped at her mother. She understood now that Jansz had tricked her again—this time into leaving her beloved leopard at his mercy—but she couldn't make any sense of her mother's words.

"Why would I agree to go to Uncle's house?"

"I'm losing patience with you, Selvi," said Mother, exasperated. "Uncle suggested this when we last visited him. He thinks that it would be better for you to stay with him and Aunty for a few weeks to learn some life skills and manners. And after the way you've been acting, I agreed."

Selvi's mind reeled. She couldn't remember discussing anything at Uncle's house, but then she hadn't been paying attention. She must have nodded her head at the wrong moment and they would have taken it as her agreement.

"Mother, I'm so sorry but I've got to go. We'll talk about this later."

"No, we won't!" yelled Mother. "You *stay right here,* Selvi, and you listen to me."

Selvi was stunned by her normally placid mother's reaction. But this was an emergency, and she'd never be able to make Mother understand.

"I'm sorry, Mother." She shook her head pleadingly but said firmly, "I don't have time to explain, but I have something very important to do."

Just then her uncle materialized from inside the house, looking incandescent with rage. "How dare you disobey your mother? I've been listening to every word. Sister, you were right to be firm with her. Leave her with me. I'll make sure she sees sense."

He seized Selvi by the elbow and dragged her toward his carriage. Selvi screamed and looked imploringly at her mother. "Please, Mother! I must go back to the mountain. Just this one last time. It's important." She was really frightened. Lokka needed her, *now.* She should never have listened to that treacherous Jansz. How easily he had tricked her! And now he held Lokka's fate in his hands.

But Mother just looked at her with sadness. That was what hurt Selvi the most: seeing the disappointment on her mother's face as Uncle pushed her into the carriage.

"Uncle," said Selvi. She had to try and talk to him, tell him how important this was. The carriage rattled up the path in the direction of his house.

He looked at her coldly.

"There's a leopard. On the mountain. They've trapped him and now they're taking him away. We need to stop them."

Uncle frowned. "Why is this any of your business?"

"Because . . . Because . . ." Uncle's face was stony. She saw that there was no point telling him anything. She'd have to think of some way to escape instead.

"Oh, never mind."

She was losing valuable time. As soon as the carriage stopped and the doors opened, she was going to jump out and make a run for it. She'd put things right with her family later. All she could think about now was Lokka. They might be taking him away right at this very moment. Her face crumpled. She hoped they hadn't got too far yet. How much could Amir do on his own?

She prayed they hadn't harmed the leopard. She knew Jansz had been told to capture him alive, but what if Lokka had put up a fight? If she didn't get to him right away, he'd be shipped off to some faraway country to be kept in a cage and gawked at.

She pushed down the sob that threatened to come out. Uncle looked at her sternly and she gazed despairingly at the passing scenery. They were climbing up the hill now, Uncle's house getting closer every moment.

When the carriage slowed down, Selvi braced herself. They clattered over the fancy gravel and came to a stop.

Selvi leaped up and pushed the door. Quick as lightning, Uncle got up and grabbed the back of her dress. "Oh no, you don't," he said as she struggled.

"Here, hold her," said Uncle to the driver, who'd come to the carriage door. He looked startled at the request, and hesitated.

"Come on!" barked Uncle, gripping Selvi's arm tightly. "Before she runs off."

"Uncle! No! Let me go," she yelled, kicking and squirming as the driver pulled her reluctantly up the steps to the house.

They swept past a surprised Aunty, Selvi screaming at the top of her lungs now as she hit out against her captor. But the driver was strong, and with Uncle leading the way, he walked her through the house, up the stairs, and down a passage to a room. "You will stay here and you will listen!" said Uncle, his face hard. "You can go home once you've learned to behave yourself and stop acting like a wild animal."

"You can't do this!" she screamed. "Mother won't allow it!"

"Well, your mother is not here, is she? And she's entrusted you to my care, so you don't get a choice." He stepped closer and shook his finger at her. "And don't you *ever* question me. I can do anything I want. I'm the *king of the mountains*."

The driver seemed uncomfortable with the situation and loosened his grip on Selvi. But Uncle took over, pushing her into the room and slamming the door. Selvi's mind filled with the image of Lokka spinning in the air inside the net as Uncle turned the key and trapped her inside.

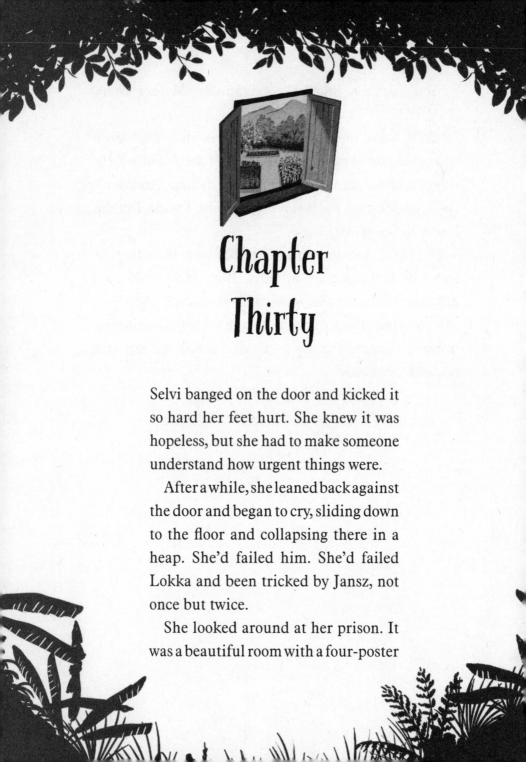

Chapter Thirty

Selvi banged on the door and kicked it so hard her feet hurt. She knew it was hopeless, but she had to make someone understand how urgent things were.

After a while, she leaned back against the door and began to cry, sliding down to the floor and collapsing there in a heap. She'd failed him. She'd failed Lokka and been tricked by Jansz, not once but twice.

She looked around at her prison. It was a beautiful room with a four-poster bed and a large carved and polished almirah on the side. Purple hand-loomed curtains framed a window. She thought it had probably been her cousin's room before she got married and left home.

Selvi took a deep breath and calmed herself down. She had to be smart, not angry. Fighting didn't work, so now she had to find a different way. She padded to the other side of the room and threw open the wooden shutters covering the window.

The room was at the back of the house, and it overlooked bright forest and, closer to the house, some vegetable patches. Yardlong beans and snake gourds grew in rectangles of black soil. It was a long way down to the ground.

Suddenly Selvi felt a spike of hope. The window was high up, but she wasn't afraid of heights. And if there was one thing she was good at, it was climbing! She hopped up to the windowsill and peered out. There was a long ledge below the window. It was a bit too thin for her liking, hardly wider than her feet. But for someone who'd climbed up a practically vertical cliff, this would be a breeze!

Selvi felt a fizz of hope as she swung one leg out of the window.

Chapter Thirty-One

Just as she was preparing to swing the other leg over the windowsill, there was a movement in the garden below, close to the house. Selvi pulled her leg back in and dropped down to the floor.

In a few moments she peeped back outside, straining out to see close to the back of the house, where she spied someone seated at a bench in a recessed courtyard.

Uncle!

Selvi groaned and ducked down again. He must have known she'd try to escape. He was keeping a very close watch on her.

She peeped out again. Uncle picked up a cup of some hot brew and poured it into a saucer, then sipped from it.

Suddenly Selvi pricked her ears. There was a banging coming from somewhere in the house, followed by lots of yelling. She crossed over to the locked door and pressed her ear to it. Sure enough, she heard the *bang, bang* again, as if someone was beating on the front door.

Uncle's voice floated up from below, calling out to someone as Selvi ran back to the window.

The driver came rushing up to him. "Sir, there's some children at the front door, making a racket. They're looking for your niece."

"*Children?*" said Uncle, perplexed, as if he'd never heard the word before. "What would they be wanting with Selvi?"

"They say they're friends of hers."

Selvi put her hand over her mouth. Friends of hers? Was it . . . ? Her heart thudded wildly. She couldn't dare hope . . .

"Chase them away," said Uncle. "They have no business coming here. If they persist, beat them."

"But, sir, some of them are tiny. There's one carrying a kitten."

Salma! Did that mean the children from school were here? To get Selvi? To help Lokka? Her heart felt so full she could cry.

"Do I employ you to question me?" said Uncle. "Go and do as I say."

The driver went off at once to the front of the house. Selvi hoped the children would disperse quietly. She felt heartened that the driver seemed reluctant to hurt them. She really had to do something to get out now. She had friends ready and waiting to help. She felt so useless and frustrated up here in the room.

A few minutes later the driver was back to tell Uncle that the children were now sitting quietly in front of the house, refusing to leave.

Her uncle started shouting at the driver again, before she heard his chair scraping back. He let out an exclamation of annoyance before setting off down the hill. She wondered why he wasn't going around to the front to send the children away.

Selvi peered cautiously out of the window. Uncle was walking past the vegetable patches to where a figure was standing in the distance. It looked like the person was waiting for Uncle. Great! While Uncle was distracted, Selvi could seize her chance to get out of the house. She hopped out to the ledge at once.

The wind whipped at her as she moved slowly along the ledge, her feet shuffling and fingers gripping onto the window. Climbing mountains was much easier than smooth walls! She intended to move all the way to the left and then around the side of the house, hoping to come across something she could use to help her climb down. She cast a quick look at her uncle's distant figure as she edged along.

There was an expanse of wall between her window and the next one, and Selvi reached across it to grab the windowsill. She hoped no one was in the room.

She pulled herself over to the window. It was open, but Selvi was in luck and the room was empty. She paused and took a small rest, breathing in deeply and bracing herself to keep going.

Uncle's voice suddenly boomed out as if he was arguing with the man he'd met, and Selvi turned to see what was going on. At the exact same moment Uncle turned too, and in a blind panic Selvi threw herself in through the window.

She lay on the floor for a moment, hoping against hope that he hadn't seen her, and trying to understand what she'd just witnessed. It was something shocking, something she wasn't quite sure was real. Something that changed everything she knew.

She raised her head slowly over the windowsill and looked out cautiously. She stared hard at the man Uncle was talking to.

This time there was no doubt in her mind. It was Jansz.

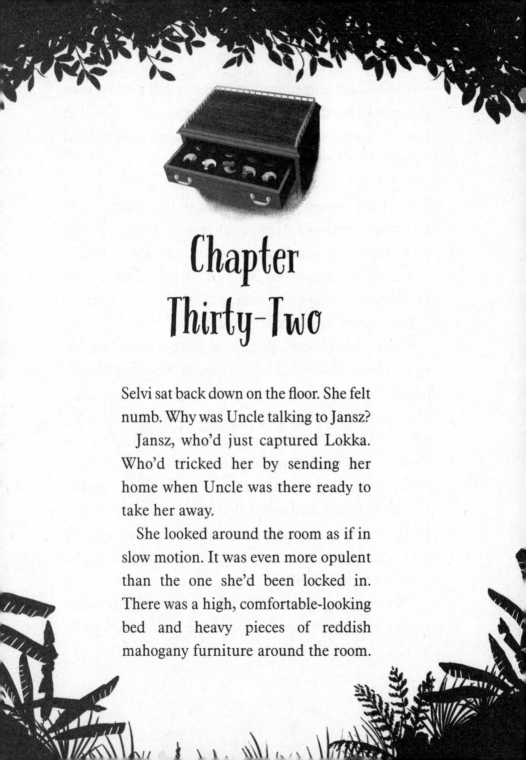

Chapter Thirty-Two

Selvi sat back down on the floor. She felt numb. Why was Uncle talking to Jansz?

Jansz, who'd just captured Lokka. Who'd tricked her by sending her home when Uncle was there ready to take her away.

She looked around the room as if in slow motion. It was even more opulent than the one she'd been locked in. There was a high, comfortable-looking bed and heavy pieces of reddish mahogany furniture around the room.

Her eyes were immediately drawn to a tall cabinet with three brass-handled drawers standing against the wall in front of a strip of brightly patterned rug. A thick gold bracelet sat on top of it.

This was Uncle's room.

Selvi got up and walked slowly to the cabinet. Her feet moved her toward it in deliberate steps, as if pulled by a thread she could not see or escape. The roar of a thousand leopards filled her ears as her hands closed around a brass handle and she pulled a drawer open.

The drawer was filled with claws.

Thick, curved claws. Some new and perfectly formed, ripped from young and healthy leopards. Some broken or yellowed with age. Each one belonging to a beautiful animal that had once prowled Serendib's forests. Tears fell down Selvi's face as she opened the next drawer, and the next—all three were full of boxes and boxes of claws.

So *this* was how Uncle had made his money. Leopards had made Uncle rich, and they'd paid for some of Selvi's comforts too. She held up a handful of claws and let them slip out of her fingers and on to the floor as she sobbed uncontrollably.

The door opened and Uncle stood at the threshold, staring at Selvi. "*What* are you doing, you stupid girl?" he said, coming into the room.

Selvi turned to him, her eyes bloodshot. "It's you," she said. "*You're* the boss."

Uncle grabbed her by the shoulders and shook her. "*Why* must you keep meddling in things that are none of your concern? You had no business trying to thwart Jansz, and you certainly have no business coming into this room and snooping in my affairs!" He slammed two of the drawers shut and began hastily to gather up the claws that had fallen on the floor.

At that moment, the door was pushed open. "Mother!" said Selvi. "You came."

She smiled at Selvi, but stood at the door uncertainly. "What's going on here?"

"What are *you* doing here?" Uncle yelled at her. "I don't recall asking you to come."

She flushed. "It's just— Brother, some children from Selvi's school came to speak to me. They told me a disturbing story." She stopped, her eyes falling in horror the claws clutched in Uncle's hands. "What are those?"

"Nothing. Mind your own business." He threw the claws into the drawer and shut it with a crash. One more remained on the floor and he picked it up.

"They're claws," said Selvi. "Leopard claws. One from every leopard he's killed."

Mother looked from Selvi to Uncle. "Is this true?"

"Of course it's not true! Why would you listen to the words of an out-of-control, disobedient child like this?"

Selvi's mother shook her head. "I'm confused, Brother. But a lot of pieces of the puzzle are falling into place now."

"How dare you!" yelled Uncle. "Your child is a liar."

Mother looked at Selvi, and then she smiled. "No, Brother," she said. "*You* are the liar."

Selvi whooped before she could stop herself, and Uncle's jaw dropped.

There was a fracas on the staircase and they all turned to look out of the door. A swarm of children were running up the stairs, led by Amir and Ravindu. "What's *he* doing here?" said Selvi, glaring at Ravindu.

"Sorry," mumbled Ravindu. "Once I got involved with Jansz, I couldn't escape. I was too scared of him."

"He's with us now," said Amir as the children flooded into the room, knocking against furniture and staring around.

"Looks like your housekeeper let them in," said Mother, shrugging at Uncle.

"What's going on?" said Aunty, coming in behind them. The children spread out around the room gaping at Uncle.

"What are all of them doing here? Get out!" screamed Uncle, lunging toward the children. A lock of his hair hung down on one side messily.

Aunty saw the leopard claw clutched in his hand. Rather than looking shocked or upset, she just looked resigned.

"I should have known. All this money, just from owning that shop in town." She shook her head, and her face looked suddenly old and tired. "But I never imagined it could be *this*."

"I think we need the authorities," said Mother, looking directly at Uncle. Selvi was elated. The grown-ups were taking it seriously! This was *huge*. Not only were Mother and Aunty standing up to Uncle, they were going to turn him in.

"You're right." Aunty turned to the driver, who'd come up and was looking on at the drama. "Could you run down to town and get someone, please?"

"I'd be happy to, Madam," said the driver. "Some things need to be put right." He muttered under his breath about frightening children not being part of his job description as he went off.

"What nonsense!" yelled Uncle into the sudden silence. "Who dares talk to me like this?"

"Come on, children," said Aunty, shooing everyone out of the room. "Let's go downstairs. Uncle will stay here until he has to leave."

They swarmed out of the room, Uncle now pleading

with his wife as if he could change her mind after everything he'd done.

"Goodbye, Uncle," said Selvi, looking at him through the closing door. Before Aunty swung it shut from the outside Selvi added, "This is it. I don't think you'll be here when I get back. I've got to rescue a leopard."

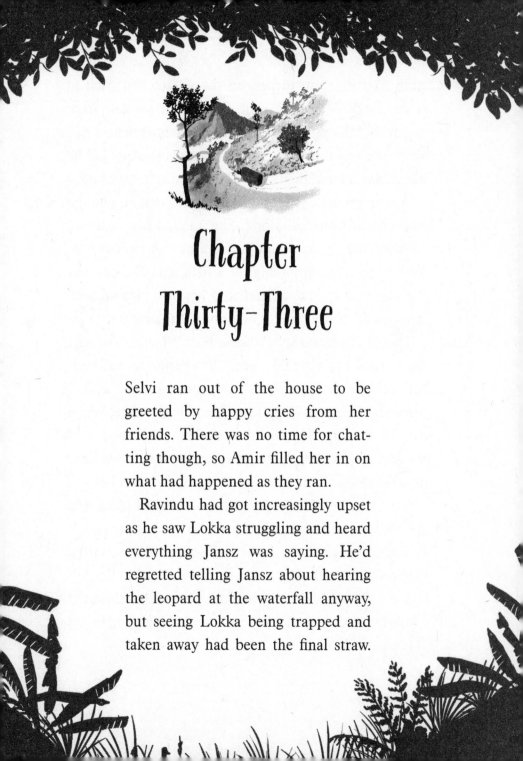

Chapter
Thirty-Three

Selvi ran out of the house to be greeted by happy cries from her friends. There was no time for chatting though, so Amir filled her in on what had happened as they ran.

Ravindu had got increasingly upset as he saw Lokka struggling and heard everything Jansz was saying. He'd regretted telling Jansz about hearing the leopard at the waterfall anyway, but seeing Lokka being trapped and taken away had been the final straw.

Amir and Ravindu turned on the villain and tried to rescue Lokka, but to no avail. They ran to get help from Priyanka. Minoli was around and she wanted to help too. Very soon, word spread among the entire class that Lokka was in danger and they were all ready to help save him.

"I even brought scissors," said Salma, listening to the story as they hurried along. She handed her kitten to another child to hold and pulled a pair out of her bag. They looked much too big for a little girl like her, but she snapped them open and shut happily, pleased with the sound. "So we can cut him out of the net."

They'd all gone to Selvi's house first. When Selvi wasn't there, Amir had feared the worst. Selvi's mother had been bemused to see all of Selvi's classmates calling for her when she'd never even had one friend over before. When Amir had heard that Uncle had taken Selvi away, he'd become suspicious of how Jansz had known to send her home at the exact time her uncle was waiting for her.

Amir had told Mother everything. About Lokka, and Selvi's bond with him, about how she was determined to save her leopard from Jansz, and how he had outsmarted her in the end. Mother had sent them ahead to Uncle's house and she'd followed behind. Once Selvi knew the whole story, she asked, "Where are we going? Where did you last see Jansz?"

"At the waterfall," said Amir. "Right where you left us. It took a while for the cart to arrive. They drugged Lokka before they could load him in. We tried to stop them but couldn't."

"Let's go back there," said Ravindu, "and see if we can trace which way Jansz went."

"Actually, we don't need that," said Selvi. "He was at the back of the house while you were all sitting at the front. Uncle was mad at Jansz for coming, I think. It sounded like he was giving him a good scolding. He definitely didn't want to be seen with him."

"Oh yes!" said Amir. "Didn't you say that he saw Jansz and Liyanage near your house that first time and he told you to keep away from them?"

Selvi laughed. "He's the boss. I guess he likes to keep his hands clean by not appearing to associate with such people. No wonder no one has ever suspected him of doing anything like this. It was a shock to his own household."

"Cart tracks!" said Ravindu from ahead, where they'd just reached the narrow road. "Look, Selvi. Lokka must have been taken this way!"

Selvi hurried over. She bent low and found deep tracks in the soil. This must have been where Jansz stopped the cart to speak to Uncle.

"Let's follow it to the road," she said. "He'll be on the way to the port. He can't have got very far!" She was very thankful for the perilous state of the mountain paths, where driving a cart was a slow and laborious process. They still had a shot at finding Lokka!

"Let's go, everyone!" shouted Selvi. "Come on, we can't let him get away."

All the children gave war cries and raced up the path. They sped along, scattering langurs and narrowly avoiding a puzzled mountain shrew.

"Look!" said a child at the front, stopping and pointing into the distance.

Selvi and the others skidded to a stop. There was Jansz's cart, bouncing down the mountainside on the road below. They'd found Lokka!

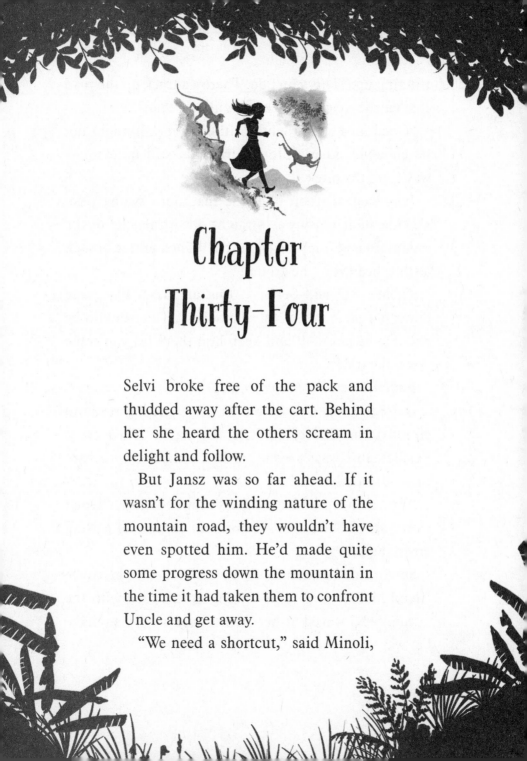

Chapter Thirty-Four

Selvi broke free of the pack and thudded away after the cart. Behind her she heard the others scream in delight and follow.

But Jansz was so far ahead. If it wasn't for the winding nature of the mountain road, they wouldn't have even spotted him. He'd made quite some progress down the mountain in the time it had taken them to confront Uncle and get away.

"We need a shortcut," said Minoli,

running up. "This won't do. There's a track up the road that cuts through. Maybe we could try that."

"Good idea," said Selvi. "Although it still might not be enough." They were frustratingly still quite some way from the track.

Just then, a troop of toque macaques swung past, making their noisy way straight down the side of the mountain and jumping from tree branch to tree branch as they headed to the ground.

"That's it!" said Selvi, getting an idea. "I'm going down the same way as those monkeys. That way I'll be able to cut Jansz off and keep him there till you come down the track."

Ravindu yelled, "Are you crazy?"

But Selvi was already on the edge, getting ready to climb down. She couldn't let Lokka be taken away. Besides, this wasn't even hard in comparison to bare rock or smooth walls!

Amir stopped and the others crowded close. "Don't worry about Selvi. She's more than capable of getting down there."

Selvi smiled gratefully at Amir. Salma and her little friend Mahesh were still coming up the road with the kitten. Selvi waved at her friends and started to make her way down the side of the mountain.

Chapter Thirty-Five

Selvi scrambled down the steep slope as fast as she could. She was Lokka's only hope now. It would be a while before her friends would catch up, taking the winding mountain track.

The sound of rattling cartwheels punctured the quiet surroundings. Selvi's heart soared even as she slipped, stubbing her toe painfully. She didn't care! She was so close. Just thinking about being this close to saving her leopard gave her a burst of energy.

She paused a moment to get her bearings. She could see Jansz driving the cart at top speed down the road beneath her, oblivious to Selvi crouching in the wilderness above him.

She moved quickly, getting into position. She braced herself. The cart came clattering along the road, moving closer and closer until the moment came when it passed directly below her.

Selvi took a deep breath and dropped down on to the roof of the cart. It swerved violently and Jansz yelled before righting it again. Selvi dropped to her knees on the roof and stayed still.

Jansz was looking in alarm on both sides of the cart, speeding up as he went. He craned back and looked at the path behind, the embankment to the side, and the drop on the other. Everywhere except the top of his own cart.

Selvi quietly crawled to the back. She peered over the edge of the roof, clinging on for dear life, to see what was inside.

There was a long lump laid out, covered by a thick sheet.

Lokka!

She lowered herself slowly over the back of the cart, holding on to the sides so that she didn't get thrown off.

She threw herself inside just as the wheels screeched and bounced over a rut in the road.

The lump shook with the moving cart. Selvi reached out and slowly lifted up a corner of the sheet. Lokka lay stretched out, his eyes closed and his face loose and limp.

Selvi's heart ached at the state he was in. From a free, proud animal running in the wild to a helpless creature, drugged and unconscious, and on the way to being sold. She put her hand on his coat and brought her face close to his.

He flinched at her touch, then opened an eye.

The cart bucked and Jansz grunted as he rode on. But all Selvi's attention was on Lokka. His open eye rolled listlessly and he closed it again. She stroked his soft fur through the net he was still wrapped in, now matted with patches of dried blood.

"It's me. I came back," she said.

Lokka's eyes opened and he locked his gaze on Selvi. His amber eyes stared into her dark-brown ones, and a flicker of recognition passed across them. His tail flicked.

But the drugs were powerful and his eyes closed again. Selvi had to find a way to make Jansz stop the cart and then hold him up until the others reached them. She pulled herself back up on to the top and crawled to the front, right behind Jansz. She tapped him on the shoulder and he yelled in alarm. The cart swerved around sharply to see Selvi clinging triumphantly to the roof. "You!" he yelled, his face purple with rage.

"I told you I'd be back," she said, jumping down and running to the front of the cart, blocking his way before he could start moving again.

Jansz looked around and back up the road. "That's it? Just you going to stop me, is it? Get out of the way before I run you over."

"It's finished," she said. "Your boss has been found out. We know it's my uncle."

Jansz didn't say anything, but she got the feeling he wanted to know more.

"Let's see. Right at this moment he's probably," she squinted as if trying to remember, "getting arrested. The game is up."

"Maybe for him!" Jansz snorted.

"Don't you get it? Your poaching ring has been busted open!" She had to keep him talking. Where were the others?

Jansz shrugged, seemingly unconcerned. "Why should I care? Makes no difference to me what happens to Kandaraja. Just means a bigger share of the profits for me." He laughed wheezily.

A movement behind the cart farther up the road caught her eye. Amir! The first of the children were creeping stealthily toward them.

She kept her gaze on Jansz, trying not to show her excitement. "I don't think you'll make it before the buyer sails away."

Jansz frowned as he pondered how she knew so much. But then he grinned. "Possibly. But it doesn't matter. If that happens, I can easily find a new one. The buyers will be after *me*."

Behind him, Amir, Ravindu, and Minoli were leading the pack of children. They divided into two groups at the back of the cart and suddenly appeared from both sides, startling Jansz. They flocked beside Selvi and faced the man defiantly.

Jansz snorted, wheezing again as his laugh carried on for too long. "*This is* your grand plan then? A bunch of children?"

"There are many of us, and one of you!" said Amir.

Selvi noticed little Salma and Mahesh hurrying up quietly behind the cart as fast as their legs would carry them. She prayed that Jansz wouldn't see them too, and she felt as if her heart had moved into her mouth.

"I'm not worried," Jansz said. "I don't like children. Never have. I'd be happy to run you all down."

Selvi watched out of the corner of her eye as Salma handed her kitten to Mahesh and took out her scissors. She climbed quickly into the back of the cart without Jansz having any idea of what was going on.

"You'll never get away with this!" Selvi yelled, keeping Jansz's attention on them.

Jansz shrugged. "And yet," he said languidly, "I'm the one with the leopard. Now, I'm losing patience. Get out of my way."

Selvi sneaked another look at the back of the cart where, for some reason she couldn't fathom, Mahesh had started picking up branches from the ground.

"This is your last chance to move," said Jansz, "before you get hurt."

"No!" said Ravindu suddenly. "I want to come with you!"

His outburst was so sudden and so unexpected that Selvi jumped out of her skin. But then she realized that the other children had noticed what Salma and Mahesh were up to. They were trying to stall Jansz too! "Don't be stupid, boy," said Jansz. "I've already paid you. Now, get lost."

"But I want to see you selling the leopard!" Ravindu said in a whiny voice, stamping his feet for good measure. "I helped you find it!"

Jansz was completely thrown by this idiotic behavior. From what Selvi could see, Salma had climbed down from the cart but now she was helping Mahesh to heave a big stone inside it.

"But what about me!" said Amir. "If I'd never told Ravindu about the leopard he wouldn't have even met you. So *I* should be there when the leopard is sold."

"And me!" said Minoli. "I sit in the same row as Amir in school so I have a right to see it too."

"I sit *next* to him," said another boy. "It should be me!"

"Shut up!" yelled Jansz. "I don't know what you kids are playing at but you'd better get lost before you make me mad."

Mahesh held up his tiny hand as if to say they needed just a few more minutes. Salma was scrabbling about on the ground and they were still doing something to the inside of the cart.

"Okay then, one final thing," said Selvi, hoping to steal a few moments until the children were done. "I just want to say a few words. You owe me that. And you owe Lokka that. And you owe nature that. I never wanted to part with this leopard. He was my friend and everything I ever wanted. I will never forget him till the—"

Mahesh gave them all a big thumbs-up to signal they were finished. He and Salma stepped into the tall reeds by the side of the road, disappearing from sight. "Yeah, and . . . all that stuff," said Selvi. She turned to the children. "Please step aside. He has won. It's useless."

Amir tried to hide his giggles as they all moved off to the side of the road, leaving the way clear for Jansz. He sat there for a moment, confused, then looked back quickly over his shoulder at the road before climbing down to look inside the back of the cart.

Selvi and the other children held their breath.

But Jansz just got back into his seat, glared at the children and drove off, looking completely unsettled by the whole episode.

They watched him trundle off, Selvi's heart thudding in anticipation. The cart rolled away down the road, rattling noisily, and they followed its course for a few moments as it threaded in and out of sight. As soon as they couldn't see the cart any more they ran over to where Salma and Mahesh had hidden.

The two little children came out of the tall grass with proud smiles on their faces.

"Look," said Salma, pointing.

Stretched out among the ferns, still very drowsy, was Lokka.

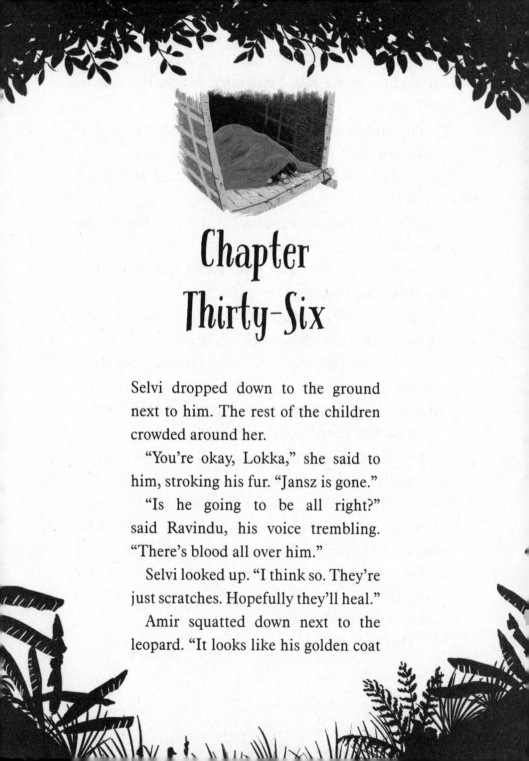

Chapter
Thirty-Six

Selvi dropped down to the ground
next to him. The rest of the children
crowded around her.

"You're okay, Lokka," she said to
him, stroking his fur. "Jansz is gone."

"Is he going to be all right?"
said Ravindu, his voice trembling.
"There's blood all over him."

Selvi looked up. "I think so. They're
just scratches. Hopefully they'll heal."

Amir squatted down next to the
leopard. "It looks like his golden coat

saved him in the end. Jansz made sure not to damage it."

Priyanka had tears in her eyes. "It was barbaric, trapping him like that."

"You did so well, Salma," said Amir. "And you too, Mahesh."

"That was such a great idea," said Selvi. "Weren't you scared?"

Salma shook her head. "No. I told you all in class, leopards don't mean us any harm."

"How did you move him?" said Ravindu. He bent down and gently touched Lokka's coat.

"That was really difficult!" said Mahesh. "We struggled so much. But we managed to wake him so he could crawl out and we didn't have to try to lift him. Then he went back to sleep."

Lokka stirred slightly. He looked up at his rescuers. "Thank you, Mahesh. And Salma. And everyone," said Selvi. The tears had started to come, but she didn't care. "I could *never* have done it without you." Priyanka smiled and patted Selvi on the back. "Wait," she said. "How come Jansz didn't realize Lokka wasn't in the cart? He must have seen he was gone, or even realized that the cart was lighter!"

"That's why we put in the branches," said Salma.

"And the stones," said Mahesh. "For some weight." Salma nodded. "We made a shape like him and put the sheet over it. So it looked like he was still there."

Mahesh began to laugh, a proper belly laugh that made everyone join in. Lokka opened his eyes again at the commotion.

"I wish we could be there to see it when Jansz gets to the port!" said Selvi, doubled up with laughter. "Poor Jansz. He's going to drive all the way there and when he looks in the cart, he'll only have some branches and stones to sell to his important buyer!"

Chapter
Thirty-Seven

A rattling on the road made the children stop laughing and look up. A stylish carriage swept by and stopped near them.

"Selvi!" said Mother, getting out with Aunty following behind her.

They stopped in shock when they saw Lokka. He was awake now but still quite languid.

"Is that—Is that . . . ?" Mother trailed off.

"Yes, Mother. This is Lokka." Selvi shifted on her haunches so Mother could see him better. "The leopard that Uncle was hunting. The one I lost, and then found, thanks to all my friends." She looked up at the children gratefully.

Mother and Aunty came closer to the leopard. The driver got off and peered at him too.

"He's beautiful," said Aunty. Selvi was thrilled at the awe in her voice.

"I've never seen one like it," said Mother, staring down at Lokka. "Just out of this world. Why is he so tame?"

"He's just sleepy," said Selvi. "Jansz drugged him, and it hasn't worn off yet."

Mother nodded. "I see. But in normal times, when he's not drugged, he hasn't tried to hurt you?"

"Never," said Selvi. "He's been like a friend to me."

"And us," said Salma. "I cut him out of his net with my big scissors, and he was a friend to me too."

Mother's eyes nearly popped out of her head. She and Aunty looked at each other.

"Where is Jansz now?" said Mother.

"He's gone off to the port to sell the leopard," said Amir. "Thinking he has Lokka in his cart!"

"I would love to be there when he discovers it," said Selvi. "I wish I could whizz myself over there somehow, but I can't."

Samadh, Uncle's driver, stepped forward. "But *I* can."

Chapter Thirty-Eight

Selvi and her friends stared at Samadh. "You mean, drive me there?" she said.

"You'd do that?"

"If Madam gives me permission, of course," he said, looking at Aunty.

Aunty looked a bit unsure. "What do you think, Gayathri?" she said to Mother.

"I don't know . . ." Mother seemed hesitant. "We've already reported Jansz to the authorities. They'll be waiting for him when he gets there."

"That's even better!" said Selvi. "We should be there to see it. Come on, Mother. Please!"

The other children made pleading faces and gestures, pressing closer around her. Salma held up her kitten as well.

"If you let me see Jansz discover there's no leopard in the cart and that we won, and then be arrested," said Selvi, "I promise I'll never climb over the roof again."

Mother laughed. "All right. You've done so much already. I can't see what harm it'll do to see it all through. And Samadh will be there."

Samadh smiled. "I'll take care of them," he said. "This carriage will take us to the port very fast. I know some quick routes to get there as well."

Mahesh whooped, and the children cheered. "Amir should go too," said Ravindu.

The other children nodded, and Amir blushed. "I'd love to," he said. "But what about Lokka?"

"Wouldn't he be safe to be left here?" said Aunty. "No animal tries to mess with a leopard."

But Selvi shook her head. "What if he's ill from the drugs? I think we should take him with us, then at least we can get help for him in the port if we have to."

Samadh grinned. "Have I just volunteered to drive two children and a leopard all the way to the port?"

"It looks like it!" said Mother.

Selvi gently patted Lokka and he moved slowly. She and Amir half carried him to the carriage, where he laid down again gratefully. He could sleep it all off on the way there. Selvi and Amir settled themselves on to the seats on either side of him.

Mother and Aunty stepped back as Samadh got ready to climb on. "We'll tell your parents where you are, Amir."

"Ready, kids?" said Samadh. "Next stop, the port!"

Chapter Thirty-Nine

There was an excited atmosphere in the carriage as they set off. Selvi was buzzing, and Amir kept looking out expectantly to see if they were nearly there. Selvi knew it was going to be many hours but she didn't mind. Lokka dozed on the floor, sleeping off the sedatives.

Once they'd come down the mountains and were on flat ground, they took the High Road. In an hour or two they were passing through the

King's City. They marveled at the royal complex as it emerged in the distance, the giant lion statue guarding the entrance to the palace's inner sanctum. Samadh stopped for a few minutes so they could stretch their legs, and he nipped out to buy them some food from the market.

"Some grand people here," said Selvi as they piled back into the carriage and Samadh passed them a box with some food.

"Let's eat on the way," he said to the children as he drove off. "We don't want to miss it."

Two girls were walking along the road, and one, beautifully dressed in red, looked at them in surprise. Her eyes widened as they moved off, and Selvi realized that Lokka had stood up sleepily and clambered to where he could see outside.

Selvi quickly gathered Lokka to her. She put him back on the floor of the carriage so that he wasn't visible from the outside. He dozed back off immediately. "She saw him, didn't she?" said Amir as they looked out.

The girl tapped the other as they walked on and said something. But when she looked it was just Selvi and Amir and she shook her head, puzzled.

"Phew!" breathed Selvi, and they smiled and waved at the girls, who waved back. "Close call," she said, leaning back against the carriage as they drove away from the King's City.

"Not long now!" called Samadh from the front. "I'm going to go off the road and we'll get there in just over an hour." The children settled in for the last bit of the journey, eating plump kolikuttu bananas and squares of milk-rice.

They were passing arid forests now, the trees woody and silver, the soil red. Crocodiles snapped at receding watering holes and a herd of wild elephants crossed the road.

"What's that noise?" said Selvi. It was a humming, like a whisper but much louder.

Amir smiled. "It's the sea! Haven't you seen it?"

"I've never been out of the mountains!" Selvi craned to catch a glimpse. The road had widened, and they were seeing other carts and carriages driving along now. They made sure to keep Lokka inside so he wasn't seen, but he was fast asleep. Selvi knew this was to be expected. Jansz must have known to drug him enough for the long journey to the port.

"I can't believe it!" said Amir. "I finally know something you don't."

Selvi laughed at his delighted expression.

Soon the horizon was all blue. A brilliant, startling

blue that arced around them on one side. Three large ships were in the sea, and the golden sandy beach was bustling with people.

Samadh drove to a halt. "I'm not going to get too close," he said to the children. "We'll have to keep the leopard hidden so I'll stay here with him. You can go off and look for Jansz. Nothing's going to happen with all these people around, of course."

They got off the cart on to the sand. Lokka was happy to stay inside; he'd looked up drowsily and seemed completely uninterested in what was going on. He crawled under a seat and stayed there.

"How do we find Jansz?" said Selvi, holding on to Amir as she faltered. Her feet sank into the soft sand. It was like walking on a bed of fine dust. The wind whipped hard but the air felt thicker than the mountains and blew sand into her eyes.

"Let's ask around," said Amir. "One of these ships must be meant to take the leopard. Let's hope it's not all over and Jansz has been arrested already."

They walked toward the water. People bustled about, and Selvi got knocked out of the way by a row of men carrying gunny sacks on their shoulders. The scent of cinnamon permeated the air in their wake. She scanned the area but couldn't see Jansz or his cart anywhere.

"Who could we ask?" said Selvi. "Everyone looks so busy and unfriendly."

As they walked close to the first ship a boy came down the gangplank, humming to himself and looking around animatedly. "Hello, hello," he said to them as he passed.

"Let's ask him," said Selvi, and they ran after the boy. He looked friendly and happy to help.

"Hi," called out Selvi to the boy, jogging behind him. He stopped and waited for them, a smile of pleasant surprise on his face.

"We were wondering," said Amir, "might you know of a merchant who wants to buy a leopard?"

"A nice one," said Selvi. "Really special. Rare."

"The leopard's here?" said the boy. He looked behind Selvi and Amir, as if he expected to see a golden-ringed leopard strolling casually after them.

This was good, thought Selvi. The boy had heard about Lokka.

"No, but, er . . ." Amir rubbed his nose. "We know the person who's bringing him, and we just want to, er . . ."

"I *could* take you to the merchant," the boy said, his mood changing at once. He waved his hands dismissively at them. "But I don't really want to. I'd love to see this leopard, but I don't approve of this animal trade.

I'm only a ship's boy, but someday when I'm captain I'd never allow that on my ship."

Selvi grinned at him. "You're our kind of person, actually. Take us to the merchant and you'll see that we only want justice served."

The boy paused a moment, and then seemed to trust their word. He nodded and gestured for them to follow. As they walked along the beach, he was chatty again. "I must admit," he said, curving his hands expressively, "I've never seen a golden leopard in my life. And there's not much *I* haven't seen. I mean, I *did* come face-to-face with a diamond-horned rhino in the Kalamanthana rain-forest that one time, but *still*, a golden-ringed leopard is something else."

Selvi looked across at Amir. She wasn't sure if the boy was pulling their leg.

He marched them toward a large sun canopy set back among coconut trees. A few people were milling about, but this part of the port was much quieter than the bustling beach near the ships. There was a table with a tray of fruit laid out and a few comfortable-looking chaise seats. A man with thick gold rings on all his fingers was lounging in one of them. It was nice and cool under the canopy. "What do you want?" said a man, coming up to them with a ream of paper in his hand.

"They've come about the leopard," said the boy, pointing to Selvi and Amir.

The man with the rings sat up. "Is it here?"

Selvi shot a gleeful look at Amir. Jansz obviously hadn't arrived yet.

"Nearly," she said boldly. "We were sent ahead to make sure everything was ready."

The merchant scoffed. He picked a rambutan from a bunch next to him, flipped it open, and popped the white round in his mouth. "I don't need messengers. I just need the goods. I'll believe it when I see it."

Just then a man came running up. He came panting into the tent and bowed low at the merchant. "It's here. The golden-ringed leopard is here. The hunter's just bringing it over."

Amir and Selvi turned. Jansz was riding triumphantly into view, bringing his cart right down the beach toward them.

Chapter Forty

Selvi slipped into the shadows silently, pulling Amir with her. They disappeared behind a knot of people who had come over to find out what was going on.

They needn't have worried about being discovered. Jansz had eyes only for the merchant. He eyed him greedily as he thumped down from the cart and swaggered up the sand.

The merchant got up from the chaise and went toward the front of the canopy. An expectant silence fell over the crowd. "This way," said Jansz, gesturing grandly toward the cart. There was a squeal and the waiting crowd surged, with the shiny-eyed merchant leading the way. Selvi and Amir went along with them.

Jansz went to the back of the cart and everyone crowded around him. "Don't worry!" he said, raising his hand. "The beast is in a net."

An excited whisper went around the onlookers. Jansz seemed to enjoy it immensely. He gave it a moment or two, then gripped the edge of the sheet.

"Ready?" He whipped off the sheet with a flourish.

Chapter
Forty-One

Everyone stared into the cart.

There was a collection of thin branches and three or four big stones. Salma and Mahesh had done good work! Selvi smiled at Amir and they tried not to laugh.

The merchant was the first to break the silence. "What is this, man? Do you take me for a fool?"

Jansz grasped one of the branches and moved it aside, muttering incomprehensibly.

"What a waste of time!" yelled the merchant. "All that talk by Kandaraja about a golden leopard! Arguing back and forth on price. And you bring me *branches?*"

"It was here! It really was!" said Jansz. "He was golden. Just like a—a mythological creature."

The merchant threw up his hands and snorted. "Mythological is right! Pah. You're a liar and an idiot." The people began to laugh.

Suddenly a few men standing in front of Selvi and Amir nodded to each other and moved to take Jansz's arms. He began to bat them away, shouting curses.

The crowd began to murmur, and Selvi turned to Amir. "It's the authorities! They've been here all along, waiting for him."

Hearing her voice, Jansz stopped struggling and turned slowly toward the children. "You again! You did this!"

Selvi shrugged. "I don't know what you're talking about, Jansz. I don't know anything about a leopard." Jansz's face contorted with rage as he lunged toward her, and the men had to wrestle him to the ground to keep him under control.

The merchant turned toward Selvi. "Wait a minute, didn't you—"

One of the men came to the merchant. "We'd like you to come with us as well. We need to have a word." The merchant turned red and tried to bluster his way out of it, but they weren't taking no for an answer.

Amir whispered to Selvi, "I think our work here is done. Let's go."

They waved at the ship's boy, who bowed to them grandly as they went on their way. They left the hubbub and walked back to the carriage, where Samadh was waiting for them. Lokka had perked up considerably, and was sitting up.

"Everything okay?" asked Samadh as they got in to the shade of the carriage.

"The best!" the children said in unison, laughing. Selvi stroked Lokka's neck. He was safe. Uncle and Jansz were both gone and wouldn't disturb him again. Nobody even believed that there was a golden-ringed leopard in existence.

Samadh began to drive off and Selvi peeked out at the scene. The place was busy and bustling, as if the whole episode with the fictitious leopard had never taken place. The ships would sail away eventually, and Lokka wouldn't be on any of them.

"Look, Amir!" Selvi said. "Jansz is being taken away."

Jansz was sitting in the back of a cart, secured with leather ties so he couldn't escape. He was still shouting about a mythical golden leopard as they swept past, although no one was listening to him, nor even paid him a glance. He lolled against the side of the cart, his expression furious as he continued to ramble to himself.

Suddenly he stopped talking and stared straight at Selvi and Amir. He straightened, his eyes still on them, blinking hard as if he couldn't believe the sight. Lokka had got up. He stepped past the children and came up to the end of the carriage, standing majestically. His golden coat glowed in the sunshine as the wind from the ocean swept through his fur and flattened his ears.

Jansz's captors ignored his shouts as he screamed and pointed at their receding carriage, and Samadh sped away on the journey back home.

Chapter Forty-Two

Selvi and Amir were both very titred. Dusk was falling and they soon dozed off. Only Lokka was awake and watchful.

He stood at the end of the carriage and looked out, and since the road was empty and no one was around to see him, they left him to it. Samadh drove on, occasionally looking over his shoulder to check that all was okay.

Selvi was deep in sleep when she felt a nudge against her leg. She drowsily put out her hand to find it was Lokka. He was pushing his head against her insistently, trying to wake her up. He rubbed against Amir too, but he was dead to the world and snoring with his head thrown back.

Selvi shifted and rubbed her eyes. They were driving past dry forests. Sticklike trees with thorny branches and drying leaves scraped against the carriage. A sloth bear walked in the distance, snuffling the ground.

"What is it, Lokka?" said Selvi. He looked at her solemnly.

She smiled at him and shook Amir awake.

"Are we back?" he said, stretching and yawning.

"No. But I think you need to see this. Lokka is telling us something."

Amir looked at Lokka. The leopard glanced out at the passing scenery, and then back at the children.

"I don't get it," said Amir. He reached out and patted Lokka.

"He's saying goodbye," said Selvi gently. Strangely, it didn't make her sad.

Amir looked at her with his mouth open. "But why? Doesn't he want to stay close to us?"

"He's a wild animal. He has his own reasons. Maybe he likes the look of these forests."

Selvi kneeled down and put her arms around her beloved Lokka. She knew in her heart that this would be the last time she touched him. He was moving on, and that was okay.

Amir hugged him too, and they sat back. The thorny landscape whizzed past, now gently darkening into twilight.

Lokka leaped gracefully from the back of the cart. He looked back briefly as a final goodbye, then sprinted away on the red soil of his new home and disappeared into the trees.

Chapter Forty-Three

A few weeks later Selvi and Amir left the schoolhouse at the end of the day with all the others. They were going swimming later with Ravindu and Minoli, but first they were taking a walk to Amir's house.

Selvi looked at the mountain path snaking upward.

"Are you thinking about the plateau?" said Amir.

"Yes. I still go there from time to time. Just out walking."

Amir nodded. "I can imagine. Shall we go now? I haven't been since that last time with Lokka."

"Of course. The binara flowers are gone now, but it's still as pretty as always. Let's go and look at the view."

"Can't believe it's been a whole month," she said as they climbed up. "Feels like so much has changed."

"Your mother must be happier." Amir struggled to keep up with her and she gave him a hand getting up a steep incline.

"She is. And so am I." She stopped to admire a bunch of bright-red maha-rath-mal flowers. "Not that I was unhappy before, but something was . . . missing."

"I'm glad Lokka's safe. Wherever he is."

"Not just him," said Selvi. "Every leopard around here too. With Uncle's arrest, his whole poaching ring was uncovered. It was spread over several parts of the island."

She looked out over the mountain range and the plains opposite. Softly undulating grassland stretched out as far as they could see, and a herd of sambar watched them with their jerky, surprised eyes. Verdant forests fringed the area in a canopy of stippled orange and green leaves. Stunted, twisting trees rose up on the edges, enshrouded in soft mist.

They came up to the plateau and stopped short at the sight.

The sun was slipping down behind the peak, framing the plateau in a fiery round glow. And gazing over his kingdom majestically stood Lokka. He turned back slightly to acknowledge their arrival and then looked again at the sun-tinged valley below.

Amir started toward him, but Selvi put a hand on his arm. He turned to her in surprise.

"Let him be," she said quietly. "I think he's finished his adventures with humans and wants to go back to being wild again."

"But won't you miss him?"

"Always," said Selvi, her throat catching. "I will never forget him."

"Nor I." Amir gazed at Lokka in awe.

"If he wants us, he'll seek us out, just like he did with me to begin with. But I know he won't anymore."

Amir looked at her. "How do you know that?"

"He doesn't have to." Selvi smiled through a mist of tears. "You know, leopards are solitary animals. And that's how . . . That's how I used to be."

Amir looked at her with understanding, giving her time to collect her thoughts.

Selvi sniffed and wiped her eyes. "I was by myself

every day on the mountains. He must have sensed my loneliness and come to me. And now he knows I don't need him anymore."

"I always thought he was the one who needed you," said Amir thoughtfully. "Because of Jansz and everything. But it looks like you both needed each other."

Selvi nodded, unable to say any more. They turned to leave, but Selvi paused for one last glimpse of her leopard.

Lokka had turned his head and was looking back at her. She knew from his expression that he'd never forget her too.

This was *his* territory, and no one would bully him out of it. His wounds were healed, and the ripped ear was the only sign of the struggles he'd been through. *Lokka*, thought Selvi, considering the name with a burst of affection as she and Amir carried on down the mountain. *He* was the boss.

After they'd gone, the beautiful leopard settled down with his head on his paws as the sun set on the true king of the mountains.

Acknowledgments

First and foremost, big thanks to Kirsty Stansfield, my editor who spots everything! This is our third outing and I've appreciated every pad of the journey. Thank you to the entire team at Nosy Crow for publishing my books so brilliantly. To Kate, Catherine, Rebecca, Sîan, Beth, Hester, Hannah, and all the crows, I'm truly grateful.

To David Dean and Nicola Theobald, thank you for a roaringly stunning cover. I don't want to sound obvious, but it does leap off the page so beautifully.

To the wonderful Joanna Moult. Thank you for all the calming chats, assurance, and advice. It's impossible to put a paw wrong with you as my agent! To my writing friends, I couldn't have done it without you. Yasmin Rahman, Hana Tooke, Az Dassu, Rashmi Sirdeshpande, Lesley Parr, Sophie Kirtley, Rachel Huxley, Hannah Gold, Catherine Emmett, and so many others for your glossy, golden loveliness.

Writing is such a solitary pursuit, I'm so glad I have a pack to turn to.

To all the librarians who've loved *Elephant* and *Whale,* especially lovely Jenny Hawke, thank you so much. To the teachers who've championed my books, a very special thank you. To Chris Tarrant, Pie Corbett, Kevin Cobane, Kate Heap, Jacqui Sydney, Scott Evans, Alex Mattimoe, Tara's Teaching, Ceridwen Eccles, Farzana Iqbal, Tom Griffiths, Rumena Aktar to name a few. To various reviewers, bloggers, and authors: Fern Tolley, Chris Soul, Leti Hawthorn, Stephanie Burgis, Tracy Curran, Emma Perry, Jo Clarke, Jo Cummins, Karen Wallee, Matt Wilson, Amy, and many others. Your support with my previous books has made the spring into book three so much easier.

To the current Year 5s of Driffield Junior School, thank you for giving me a villain! You wouldn't accept that Jansz in *The Girl Who Stole an Elephant* would continue to work for a kind monarch as it's just not in him. I think you're right, so here he is in this story, continuing his badness as you asked for.

To Katie Rushton and her Year 4s at Cheddington Combined School; the first school to hear me read from this book. Thank you for the encouraging response and for loving Selvi's story from the beginning.

A massive thank you to the booksellers who've supported my books. For voting for *Whale as* the Indie Book of the Month, and for taking my book to so many readers. Special thanks to Ayesha of MirrorMeWrite, Bronnie and Bob of Bookwagon, Mel and Nick of The

Rabbit Hole Brigg, Jo Boyles of Rocketship Bookshop, Helen Tamblyn-Saville of Wonderland Bookshop, and AJ of A New Chapter Books among others.

On the other side of the world, special thanks to Thushanthi Ponweera, Shaahima Fahim, Asha de Vos, and Tina Edward Gunawardena for your support. And as always, clawsome love and thanks to Nuha and Sanaa.

Read on to discover another great adventure
set on the amazing island of Serendib!

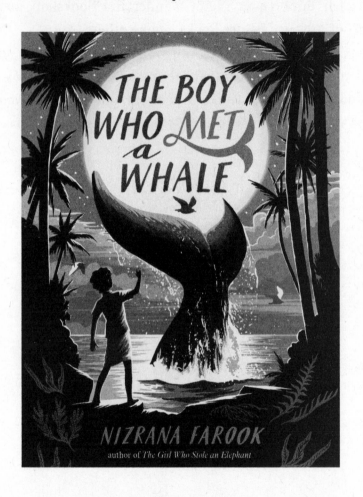

THE BOY
WHO MET
a
WHALE

NIZRANA FAROOK

author of *The Girl Who Stole an Elephant*

"An exciting and appealing page-turner."
—*Kirkus Reviews*

"A thrilling, old-fashioned treasure hunt."
—*Booklist*

THE BOY WHO MET a WHALE

Chapter One

The boy clung to the rail with a death grip as the ship lurched violently in the storm.

It was sinking.

All around him was darkness and the roar and crash of waves as the ship buckled and rain lashed down. The wind was shrill and whip-sharp. But for all the noise, the ship was empty of people. Where was everyone? The boy ran along the deck, slipping and sliding to the wheelhouse.

It was deserted.

He sprinted down the length of the ship, hurtling below deck to the captain's quarters. He pounded on the door, desperate to be heard over the sound of the thunder and the howling of the wind. But it was impossible.

The door opened suddenly and the first mate slipped out, a long leather pouch clutched in his hand. He startled when he saw the boy, and quickly hid his hand behind him.

"Sir, the storm—" began the boy, but the man shoved him aside and hurried down the passage.

The boy held on to the side for balance and stumbled into the cabin. The captain was lying in his bunk, fast asleep. The room had been ransacked: drawers were hanging open and books had been tossed all over the place. The ship listed sharply and the debris on the floor slid to one side of the room where water was pooling, creeping darkly over fallen books.

The boy froze in shock. The crew had *known* they would be sailing into a storm. Why was the captain asleep so soundly? Why was the *whole ship* asleep? Apart from . . .

He stormed out of the captain's cabin and scrambled up to the deck. A lifeboat had been lowered into the sea, and the first mate was getting ready to climb down, accompanied by a man the boy recognized as the ship's cook.

He stared at the men, a cold fear clamping around his heart as the rain soaked through him. "Marco!" he screamed. "What did you do? Did you *drug* them?"

The first mate looked back and shrugged, not even bothering to deny it.

Rain pelted the men as they prepared to get in the boat. Something snapped in the boy, and he raced toward them and plucked the leather pouch from the first mate's pocket.

Yelling, the men gave chase as the boy sprinted away down the ship. Lightning lit up his running figure. The ship groaned and shifted. The men stumbled and one fell as the boy doubled back, jumping over the fallen man and speeding past his furious companion. The first mate took out a knife that flashed silver in the gloom of the night. He ran fast, closing in on the boy as water filled the deck and crept up his ankles.

It was over. The ship was going down, and it was too late to save anyone. The boy wailed in anguish as he threw himself over the side and into the lifeboat. The ship tilted and groaned, making a huge cracking sound as it broke apart. The men ran to the railing and yelled at the boy, but the rain blotted out everything as he rowed swiftly away. The last he saw of the ship was it careening jerkily off course.

The boy screamed into the wind and wept for his lost friends.

Chapter Two

The baby turtle scuttled down the golden beach, wet and gritty with sand. Bit by bit scores of others emerged, their shiny black bodies, flailing limbs, and beady eyes glinting in the early-morning sun. They scampered toward the water, their little legs scuffling over the freshly turned-up sand. A bale of tiny turtles—all eager to make their first meeting with the sea.

Razi laughed as he ran after them, careful not to step on any of the little creatures. The sight never failed to amaze him and lift his spirits. He'd seen it a hundred times, coming early to this stretch of beach to watch the newly hatched turtles running into the sea at sunrise. There was a white one among them, an albino turtle, the pattern on its back etched out in shiny black lines. It was lagging behind and in danger of getting lost.

"Go on! Go, your friends are leaving!" called Razi. He knew not to touch it and so he hoped his voice would cheer it on instead. Sure enough, the white turtle perked up and scuttled after the others.

Overhead a yellow-beaked ibis wheeled past. Razi kept an eye on it in case it tried to attack the babies.

The sea was a grayish blue, deepening gradually to a brilliant turquoise with the rising sun shining on the waves. Coconut trees fringed the beach, their wiry trunks twisted like swaying cobras.

Standing on the shoreline, Razi watched in awe. A wave came in, drenching the baby turtles as they swarmed up to meet it. They hopped into the water, greeting it playfully. Razi held his breath. This part always worried him. The turtles looked so little and fragile. But the whole lot of them swam away happily, dots of black on the rolling blue waves surging into the great ocean.

He sat cross-legged on the sand and watched them bob away. They disappeared quickly, swimming away to their new lives. He knew that turtles always came back to the very same beach they were born in to lay their own eggs. So someday when Razi was an adult he could be back here and see the babies of one of these same turtles.

It was a lovely feeling. But it couldn't completely dislodge the sadness that dimmed Razi's world, no matter how much the sun shone and waves danced.

The sun rose higher and prickled his skin. Then he saw something bobbing in the water. Something dark.

Razi squinted into the horizon. The turtles were all gone, but this was too big to be one of them anyway.

Whatever it was, it was heading toward land.

The sea glittered a brilliant, sparkling blue now, and the dark object swirled closer and closer to the shore with every wave.

It was a boat.

Razi stood up. This wasn't a fishing boat like the ones on Serendib. This boat was plain and simple, with no sail or outrigger, and, as it moved closer, Razi saw it had some strange lettering etched on the side.

Foreign letters, thought Razi excitedly. Where had the boat come from?

About the Author

NIZRANA FAROOK was born
and raised in Colombo, Sri Lanka,
and the beautiful landscapes of her
home country find their way into
the stories she writes. She graduated
from Bath Spa University with an
MA in Writing for Young People
and lives in England with her
husband and two daughters.

Follow her on Twitter @NizRite
and visit her on the web at
NizranaFarook.com